Nicole Smith was first published when she was twelve in the local paper for a science fiction short story called 'Just Another Day In Space'. Since then she has realised that there are no days in space. *Sideshow* is her first book.

www. nicolemariesmith.wordpress.com

SIDESHOW

NICOLE SMITH

First published in Seizure by Xoum in 2014

Xoum Publishing
PO Box Q324, QVB Post Office,
NSW 1230, Australia

www.seizureonline.com
www.xoum.com.au

ISBN 978-1-922057-97-6 (print)
ISBN 978-1-921134-24-1 (digital)

Cataloguing-in-publication data is available from the
National Library of Australia

Internal design and typesetting © Xoum Publishing 2014
Cover design by Zoë Sadokierski

Edited by Patrick Allington

Viva La Novella 2 was made possible through the generous support of

For John

Belo Horizonte

It's a gorgeous day to touch the sky.

In Brazil we put the contents of a small flower shop in our wigs so we can toss pretty relics for grandmothers to turn over in their hands after we have gone. The gig is in an enormous field where they fly kites across the road from the lucky people's houses. You can tell they are the lucky people because of the broken glass lining the edge of their fences.

The show is muscular and it's a sensual crowd and we speak to a thousand strangers with our bodies. Our imprint is left, written on the wind.

When we descend, they are upon us. It is as if we can heal the sick. The little boys crowd around us especially close. One boy is learning English. He can say, 'My name is . . .' He places a hand on his chest and says, 'My name is Sabastiao Fernando.' I write lots of love to Sabastiao Fernando and he introduces each kid holding out a scrap of paper in an unwashed hand. Sabastiao Fernando points to a tall boy in short shorts.

'My name is Miguel Campos Santos.' I draw a picture for Miguel Campos Santos. Sabastiao Fernando points to another little fellow.

'My name is Jose Eduardo Taveres Melo Silva.'

I get Sabastiao to spell out his name. Jose has no paper so I use his arm. Jose Eduardo Taveres Melo Silva is transfixed by the letters appearing along his delicate limb. I draw a love heart to dot the i. The kids walk back with us to the dressing room. Men pat us on the back and women say, '*Obrigada, muito obrigada.*' We pause the procession to pose for pictures with pretty families who put their arms around us. And everyone's looking at me. Everyone loves me. This piece of me, this smallest part of me projected like a shadow puppet on the back wall of people's minds. The kites dance in the empyrean and I can smell popcorn.

—

I don't want to take the costume off. I want to be a deity forever. I want to bask in the love of a thousand faces. I spin around like a small girl. My skirt spirals in the vortex. This drug, this addiction, this distraction from my stillborn life, this is what I do.

I catch myself in the mirror and suddenly I'm Miss Havisham in a long velour dress and a fright wig. I see the crone in the maiden's gown caught in a single moment, calcifying in the best of times until it becomes the worst of times meanwhile missing all of the other times: the good times, the fair-to-middling of times, and the times when nothing much seems to be happening at all. Everything you love discards you in the end. Even gorgeous days slip away through the horizon. All I can be sure of is that I am running out of time.

I take off the wig and I'm left a woman with flat hair and a smudged face.

Begin again

I have to pick up the others on the way to the airport. I leave my place two hours before check-in which is two hours before take off. I hate being late. Not everyone hates being late.

The taxi driver is a wiry guy of indeterminate age with a beard. A career cabbie. He helps me with my luggage. I've packed my case, taking only the portable, the foldable and the light, leaving enough space to fill later with all the beginnings, the promise, the life still to be led. I can be anyone. No burden of history creating arthritic relationships. No ends, just interruptions and beginnings. The taxi smells of laboratory apple scent.

We're slicing through the streets on the wrong side of the speed limit when the driver comments on the weather.

'Nice weather we're having.'

'This town doesn't have its own weather. It does impersonations of other climates. When we have four seasons in one day, that's just the weather showing off.'

The driver appraises me in the rear-view mirror for a moment. I change the subject. 'So, what's it like being a taxi driver?'

'Well, you need patience and skin like a crocodile.

Some of the things that get said to you . . . I just agree with whatever they're saying. Nod along. It's much easier.'

'Do you get more tips that way?'

'You do.' He smiles a little. I smile with him.

'If you're going to be confrontational, then they're going to come back at you. Especially with a bit of soup in them.'

'So you just nod along?'

'Yeah.'

'What's it like driving a yellow cab?'

He thinks for a moment. 'It's sort of like wearing a yellow tie.'

We pull into Edmund's driveway. He's not waiting out the front. I knock on the door. It takes a long time before I hear someone at the lock. Edmund is in his underwear.

'You ready?'

He looks at me.

'You're not ready, are you?'

He shakes his head.

'How about I go pick up the Prince and come back for you?'

He nods. He gives me his sweetest smile. He gently closes the door. I can hear running down the hall.

—

'You travel much?' asks the driver.

'I do.'

'You like it?'

'I do.'

'What do you like about it?'

'I like hanging around airports.'

'You do?'

'Not much.'

The cab driver regards me briefly. He looks a touch hurt.

'I don't know,' I say, trying to take the question seriously, 'a last chance to see. I may as well have a look at it all before the world ends. May as well have a look at all the monuments to human endeavour before they fall. Walk in the final remnants of the natural world. See all the fine things that used to be forests. Dine in the dying light on the last of the oceans sheltering on an elegant patio with a stunning vista as the earth breathes its last.'

'I see,' says the driver.

I briefly wonder if I haven't said too much, the way you sometimes do when you confide in strangers. And yet I keep talking.

'When you realise that your life is worthless you either commit suicide or travel.'

'You really should cheer up.'

'I am cheerful. I just won the lottery.'

'Win much?'

'I won the chance to stand in a dark cave and watch the sun come up for seventeen minutes.'

'You won the Newgrange lottery.'

This cabbie knows his Megalithic passage tombs.

'That's the one. My ticket was chosen out of forty thousand. I'm one of the lucky ones who will spend winter solstice in Ireland, at dawn, standing in a cruciform chamber with a corbelled roof to see a beam of light illuminate a passageway falling two metres short of the back wall.'

'The light falls short of the back wall because the tilt of the earth's axis has changed since it was built five thousand years ago,' says the driver.

'That's right.'

'Congratulations.'

'Thanks.'

'So why Newgrange in particular?'

'Why do we do anything, really? I entered a lottery on a whim and I won it on a whim.'

In the rear-view mirror, the cabbie doesn't look convinced.

'I want to see ancient architecture and a trick of the sun.'

The cabbie takes his eyes of the road to look at me again. I try once more.

'Maybe the ancients left a message I want to hear. And maybe I want to mark the moment. It's impossible to remember all the moments of your life. But I'll remember this one and mark it against the moment I stood in the doorway, downstairs outside the laundry, just a kid in a small town on the Tropic of Capricorn. The thing about the Tropic of Capricorn is that it marks the most southerly latitude at which the sun can appear directly overhead during the December solstice. You don't cast a shadow at noon on one day of the year. I was looking at a daddy-long-legs spider and neither of us had a shadow. I marked the moment to measure my life against. This moment in Newgrange, pretty much on the other side of the globe, can be a moment like that. I will experience a moment in space-time set on an arbitrary set of coordinates, watch the sun come up and mark my life against the time I stood next to a spider without a shadow.'

'It will probably be very cold.'

'I packed an extra cardigan. Just here.'

The cabbie turns into the Prince's street.

The Prince is sitting on his verandah drinking with

friends but he's packed and mostly tidy. He brings his beer into the taxi.

'You are outrageous. You know that, don't you?' I say as he climbs into the back seat.

'It was a big night. My going away party. Going to sleep it off on the plane. Where's Edmund?'

'Wasn't ready. Going to pick him up now.'

'Ah, Edmund,' says the Prince and looks out the window.

'Where you all going?' asks the cabbie.

'Everywhere,' says the Prince.

'An international man of mystery then?'

'We're going on tour,' I say. 'James Bond here is an acrobat. He's very quick on his hands.'

'Very good.'

'What's it like being a cabbie?' asks the Prince.

'Well, the world comes to you. Chinese, Japanese, Timorese, Bengalese.'

'Right.'

'Danes, Ethiopians, Dutch.'

'That's a lot of people.'

'Cubans, they're always smoking, Bolivians, Cambodians, Canadians, Colombians, Catholics, Hungarians, Palistinians, Mexicans, and the Swiss. They all come through the car from all over the world. You get that every day. Every single day your life is different.'

'Cool,' says the Prince and takes a swig of his beer.

—

No sign of Edmund as we pull up to his house for the second time today. I jump out and go to the door. It only takes one knock this time. Edmund's special friend Elsie answers the call. She's a sweet, pretty, young thing – all black hair, luminous skin and lovely manners.

'He's ready now,' she says.

Edmund appears, carrying his things. We walk to the taxi. Edmund stands on the footpath and takes a while to say goodbye to his special friend Elsie. The farewell becomes almost inappropriate for a public street. Eventually he jumps into the back seat.

'You got everything? Passport, tickets?' I say, trying not to use my mum voice.

Edmund checks his pocket. Then he looks through his jacket. Then he rummages through his bag.

'Guys, I've left my passport inside the house.'

I look at my watch. 'Well, hurry up then.'

'Yeah but . . . my keys are sitting next to the passport inside the house.'

The house, which is now securely locked. Elsie, who is still standing on the kerb, doesn't have keys either.

'Edmund,' I say, using the tone we all take with Edmund in times like these.

'You go pick up the Princess and I'll go and break into my house.'

—

The Princess eventually answers my knock.

'I'll just get my bags.'

She has a lot of bags. A lot of big bags. A lot of very big bags. And they all match. A pink floral pattern that baffles the eye. The driver uses his secret cabbie powers to get them all in the boot.

—

For the third time today, we pull into Edmund's driveway. He is standing forlornly in the front yard.

'I can't get in.'

The cabbie suddenly becomes action man, takes off his seatbelt and gets out of the car.

'Let me have a look.'

He takes a piece of wire from under the seat. Edmund follows him nervously.

After a short while, they return. Edmund has his passport. He says goodbye to his special friend Elsie a little more quickly this time and we pull away from the house for surely the very last time. Elsie waves until we are out of sight.

'Edmund,' demands the Prince, 'what's going on, dude?'

'Lost track of time.'

'Lost track of time?'

'I was having sex all morning and lost track of time. You know what it's like.'

The Prince doesn't look at all pleased.

'So what's it like being a taxi driver?' says Edmund in a voice that is a little too loud.

'Well, it's a bit like . . .'

The Princess, sitting in the front seat of the taxi, chooses this moment to put on the radio. It's tuned to a classical music station.

'I like this song,' says the Princess. 'I used to do my ballet barre to this song. Who is it?'

'It's Bach,' says the driver. 'Invention Number One.'

This cabbie knows his eighteenth-century composers. We listen for a while as we watch the familiar landmarks of the city recede into the distance.

'I like classical music,' confides the Princess to her

captured audience. 'Did you know that Joanne Sebastian Bach is the most famous composer in the world?'

'You don't say,' says the cabbie, nodding.

'Yes. He enriched the German style with a robust contraception technique but he still had twenty children.'

'Really?' says the cabbie, nodding some more.

'Yes. He used to practise on an old spinster.'

'Don't you mean spinet?'

'No. Spinster.'

Now everyone is nodding.

—

We're not late after all. We join the others waiting to check in. The Chancellor is at the front of the line demanding that we all hand her our passports. She is a heavy, officious woman who used to work for the public service in a particularly infuriating part of the sector.

'Quickly now,' she says, counting the slender books in her hands. 'Edmund, where's your passport?'

Edmund is searching through his bag. He looks just about ready to climb into it. And then Edmund has a thought. 'Maybe I left it at the coffee stand.'

'Well, go get it. The flight is not going to wait for you.'

Edmund scampers away. The Chancellor looks at the girls working behind the desks at check-in.

'I hope we get a girl who can speak English. I don't want to start the mime show before we've even left the airport.'

And here's the thing, the Chancellor doesn't like foreigners. She's our tour manager.

The Generalissimo is standing behind her. He is a very short man and he's 'over it'. He's been 'over it' for years.

He doesn't like performers or touring or showering. He carries a hip flask. I think he's always drunk. He's our safety officer.

The Generalissimo says a begrudging hello to my cheery greeting and settles back into silence. I struggle in the silence and so try to fill it with words.

'These queues are long, aren't they? Makes you wish you were in business class, doesn't it? Straight up to the counter and then straight down to the lounge for the catering and the newspapers. After that it's all first on the plane, drink on arrival and real cutlery and china plates. And those little comfort bags with the perfume and moisturisers. When I get off a plane I always check to see if anyone in business class has left their complimentary comfort bag. Sometimes I'm lucky. Sometimes they haven't even been opened. The trick to taking a complimentary comfort bag from business class is to do it as if it is the most normal thing in the world to do. And quickly. Quickly is important. You have to get in and out before an air hostess notices.'

I try to stop talking. Eventually I do.

The Lady In Waiting is waiting next in line standing beside one of the biggest suitcases I have ever seen in my life. She could be transporting a body in that thing. The Lady wears a tracksuit, which has a glittering 'Honey' emblazoned across her bottom. She has long, jet-black hair. Underneath a full face of make-up, she looks like she needs a steak. She shows her teeth to me like someone who is unused to smiling.

And then there is me. The Courtesan. I'm just happy to be invited.

We are the Kingdom of Nobodies. Sometimes we visit real royal courts and entertain them before dinner.

Other times we play to the multitudes gathered in town squares, at festivals, in parks, on traffic islands and sometimes behind the basketball courts. Free for the people. Pleasant distractions. Diversions for all.

The Princess prances up to me. 'Thank you for letting me borrow this book,' she says.

The Princess chooses this moment, as we stand in line waiting to travel overseas for a very long time, with a limit of twenty kilograms for each person, to return the book she has borrowed from me. She hands me *Arabian Nights*. The book is a very heavy, hardback tome in large print with brass corners. I consider telling her where to put it. I decide instead to leave it on a bench before I go through customs.

'Thank you, Princess.'

Edmund rushes up clutching his passport.

'Found it. A nice girl behind the counter put it aside. I got her number as well.'

'Well give it here,' says the Chancellor.

'What? The phone number?'

'No, your passport.'

'I want a window seat,' says Edmund.

Edmund won't be getting a window seat. If the Chancellor can manage it, she'll get him in the middle of a row of four, just outside the toilets.

A certain sentimentality colours the beginning of a new tour. Infamous stories get retold, indignities revisited, fun recaptured and slanders brought up to date. Everyone's brimming with excitement. This never gets old.

'Who are we flying?' asks Edmund.

'The Singaporeans,' says the Prince.

'Great: ever helpful, cute-as-a-button hostesses, movies on demand and enough legroom.'

'Yeah, better than the Dutch. No legroom, no personal TV and only cheese sandwiches to eat.'

'Or the Germans, who make you get your own drinks from down the back and the hostesses can speak all the languages in the world but they don't want to speak to you.'

'Or the Americans,' says the Princess, joining in, 'who don't let you drink but you're welcome anyway and thanks for that smile. They have old air-waitresses.'

'Well, as long as it's not the Australians,' says Edmund. 'The disciplinarian airline. Giant male stewards with big hands who never let you leave your seat even to go to the toilet and you get in trouble if you talk during the safety demonstration. The "Shut Up and Keep Still Airline". Those planes are run like convict ships.'

'What do you never leave the country without?' asks the Prince, changing the conversation to pleasanter things.

'A travel wallet, says Edmund, 'ideally leather with a coin purse for odd currency. Look at my wallet. It contains bits of paper. You just show these bits of paper to people and they let you get on a plane. It's magic.'

'Luggage on wheels,' adds the Lady. 'Backpacks are for bushwalkers.'

'Power adapters for the whole world,' says the Prince.

'Good boots, party dress but never, ever, hula-hoops,' I say.

'I take my teddy bear,' says the Princess. 'He's called Rufus. Would you like to meet Rufus?'

The Lady decides to save everyone from meeting Rufus with a confession.

'I take everything I can from the hotel room. I take soap, shampoo, conditioner, combs, toothbrushes, razors, cotton balls, sewing kits, notepaper, matches, shower caps, bibles and a bathrobe if they have one.'

Edmund does too. 'Yeah, I do too,' he says. 'Some of those hotels in France you have to bring your own soap. Touring like this is like playing a computer game where you have to pick up swords and small elves to use for your next challenge but for me, it's the antiseptic wipes from the plane and those little packet snacks. I never pack a towel.'

'We know,' says the Prince.

'Next,' says the woman behind the counter.

In the stampede for the desk everyone begins the plaintive cry, 'Aisle seat? Can I have an aisle seat on an exit?' The Princess knocks my phone out of my hand in her rush to the front of the line. A shadow behind me catches it before it hits the ground. I'm momentarily impressed by the quick reflex action. The man winks at me. I don't know if I approve of winking. Makes me check to see if I still have my purse. The man is part of what looks like a band. Behind him stand six young men, all with their original hair, wearing the secret high heels of men.

'Thank you,' I say.

He winks again. Maybe he has something in his eye.

'Pleasure,' he says in an accent I can't quite place with only a single word.

I turn back to the check-in counter. Edmund and the Prince are trying to get upgraded to business class, the Generalissimo is heading out for a cigarette, the Chancellor is struggling to get a suitcase onto the scales and the Lady is accusing the Princess of pinching her. I take my place in the chaos.

—

I do up the seatbelt. Let the boredom begin.

I'm not a good flyer. Some people say they love the peace and quiet and not having to answer the phone but for me it's like being in an old people's home where the only thing to look forward to is the next meal.

Someone is making a disturbance a couple of rows behind me. I turn around. It is the Princess. Her distinctive voice fills the plane.

'How dare you put your seat back!'

A man's voice replies but quietly enough so that I can't hear his response. But he does sound cross.

'If you want more room then you should have travelled business class!' screeches the Princess.

Hostesses converge on the incident from what seems like every corner of the plane. I can't hear what they are saying but the tone is clearly conciliatory.

'I don't see why I should move,' yells the Princess. 'He should move. Make him move. I like my seat.'

The hostesses murmur politely.

'I'll only move if you upgrade me to business class.'

The polite voices don't sound like they can accommodate this request.

'Well I'm not moving then. I'm not. I'm not. I'm not!' It sounds like the Princess is stamping her feet.

I hear someone else shuffling to their feet. I look around again. It is the man I assume was sitting in front of the Princess. He follows the hostess down the aisle. He looks relieved.

———

After dinner I take the coffee spoon from the tray and put it into my bag. I take a coffee spoon from every flight.

I can't help it. The security guards at airports don't seem to mind. Except the time I took the whole set of cutlery and the knife came up on the X-ray. I was given a very thorough patting down. And I didn't even catch his name.

—

I'm still sitting on a plane. Seven hours into thirteen. I'm having violent fantasies involving my colleagues in seats 24, 65 and 18 and all of the other passengers, especially the sookie fat man who wouldn't swap seats with me so I could have the aisle which would mean he could sit next to his wife. I have to sit next to her. She is a pale-eyed woman who is wearing as many patterns as she can in a single outfit. The patterns are in constant border skirmishes with each other. Her hands are two white snails corseted by gold bracelets. The hillside of her flesh is avalanching into my seat. I am being invaded by the immoral continent of her body. I've had three people in quick succession point their bum at me and it was like looking into their souls. I can't die in a plane crash. I can't die in a room full of people.

The joys of sleeping on planes

There are none.

São Paulo

The me, that is not really me, but much better look-ing, gazes back at me, from the mirror.

'Wonderful show,' flutes the Duke. 'Especially you, darling.' And he places a heavy hand on my shoulder.

'Thank you.'

'See you out there.'

And the Duke disappears out of the dressing room door.

I smooth my face to grey.

—

The face erased and costume discarded, I find the Duke taking apart the rigging. The Duke has been with the show since it began years ago. He's a dark-eyed man in his forties, long and lean and quick. His eyes dance with mischief like Hermes. Maybe he is Hermes come to earth to find entertaining diversion among the mortals. I sometimes think so. He hands me a shifter. I start to loosen bolts.

'Why are we doing this again?' I say.

'Because it makes people smile.'

'Is that all?'

'That, and the travel's good.'

'Speaking of travel, do you want to go to Newgrange for the winter solstice? Do the last show in Galway and go from there?'

'I do love a chambered cairn. When is it?'

'Twenty-first of December.'

'I don't know. Last show in Galway is the twentieth. Can we make it to the fairy mound on time?'

'I've got it all worked out.'

'Splendid.' The Duke frowns into his work. 'Have you seen the Generalissimo?'

'No.'

The Duke's frown deepens. And then something about a difficult bolt makes me say more than I mean to say out loud. 'I don't think the Generalissimo's up to the job. I suspect he drinks in the morning.'

'The Office,' says the Duke, coiling rope, 'in its infinite wisdom, has decided that he is up to the job. And the Office has financial problems. I don't believe it's ever been this bad. The Office says they can't afford to replace him.'

'Only forty-two shows to go.'

'Last one to fall from the rig is a rotten egg.'

I smile but I feel scared. Genuinely frightened.

'Cheer up,' says the Duke, and his eyes sparkle. 'I have the most delightful idea.'

The Duke, a veteran of many tours of duty, suggests a sly stopover in Rio just because we can. He's had a major altercation with the Generalissimo and war has now been officially declared. There were open hostilities during the set-up.

Someone swore. 'For fuck's sake, you fucking fuck.'

And then someone called someone a name. 'Oh fuck off you slubberdegullion!'

And now someone's sending a complaint to the Office. Even if they're not too sure what the insult actually means.

The Duke is scornful. 'It means he smells. And I don't care if he is calling the Office. A fabulous time is the best course of action given the circumstances and we can get the flights for free.' He punctuates this with a jaunty drag upon his cigarette. I thoughtfully exhale mine.

We can get the tickets for free because our Brazilian presenter is a handsome man with a gentle manner and a soft shine for the Duke. The presenter did something with our tickets that you can only do in a developing country.

The Duke's eyes glitter. 'We have to go to Rio. It's practically just up the road. And the others will have their own good time here.'

I think of the Lady happily starving herself alone in her room, the Chancellor enjoying wringing her hands over the cost of tipping and the Generalissimo having a really nice time travelling the streets looking to score.

'Sounds like fun,' I say. 'I'm in.'

'The Prince and Edmund are coming, which will be lovely, but unfortunately the Princess overheard us talking and now she insists upon coming along.'

I look at him.

'Now, don't give me that look.'

'Not the Princess,' I say, trying not to give him that look.

'Enough, enough.'

The Duke appeals to my better nature. It takes a while.

Rio

The songs commemorating Rio De Janeiro are impossible to ignore as you descend into an impressive bay. I try to get Peter Allen out of my head but then the 'The Girl From Ipanema' starts up. I put a coffee spoon in my bag and admire the view anyway.

—

A surprisingly small-town airport. A new hotel. A nice new hotel with romantic banisters.

We can see the Redeemer far away on his hill. This great, expansive Christ opens his warm arms to us. And we only just got here.

We walk along Copacabana Beach. Everyone looks like everyone else in the world but very good-looking and mostly nude. I long to go into the water. I'm surprised. I don't like swimming all that much.

Cut back to the street and the boys are playing dress ups in a clothes shop but I have blisters that are nagging me. Through a gate, back out to the sea and I'm in my togs having such a great time in the surf. A cute boy says something to me in Portuguese. I don my prettiest smile for the occasion.

I want artefacts. I find a wooden carving of a flower with *Rio 0905, 2004 Ailton ps* carved on the back. It's the name of the man who carved it. I think.

There are birds that look like pterodactyls flying above us. We stop for coffee and fluffy dogs in fluffy Japanese girls' arms are sitting at the next table. Lithe young men tumble impossibly on the hard city street with articulate bodies. We put money in their hats and everyone dons their prettiest smiles for the occasion.

It's already dusk. We better get moving. And the drugs are coming on. We take taxis half way up the hill through a tunnel of trees. The road leaps out, shouting 'surprise' from behind curves and corners.

We take an escalator ride outdoors under the night sky and then we see him, at first, darkly, but then face to face: Cristo Redentor.

We stand in quiet contemplation for a moment.

Edmund breaks the reverie. 'I read somewhere that he's made of soapstone.'

I imagine hundreds of Brazilian men carving him out with kitchen knives.

The Duke looks at Edmund like he's smelt something unsavoury. 'He is not.'

'I'm sure he is,' says Edmund.

The Princess tests the side of the monument with her fingernail. 'Anyone got a knife?' she asks. 'I'd like to carve my name on him.'

I am beyond indignant. 'You cannot carve your name on one of the Seven Modern Wonders of the World.'

'How about keys? Anyone got a set of keys?'

Fortunately, the Duke pretends to have a religious epiphany. The kind of roll-around-on-the-ground-loudly kind of epiphany. It's profane but we laugh. People notice. We are being so naughty. We are hysterical with joy. We drop straight back down the hill for dinner.

We have just finished eating when the Princess hits a woman in the toilets. We know this because the woman follows her out and unashamedly screams at her in the crowded restaurant. It's an exhilarating anger. Her husband calms her down. It takes a while.

The Princess doesn't meet our eyes.

'I think she walked into the door or something.'

Edmund calls for the bill. *'Canta, por favor! Canta, por favor!'*

The waiter hesitates, uncertain. Clears his throat. 'Are you sure, sir?'

'Edmund,' says the Duke under his breath, 'a *conta* means the bill. You're asking the waiter to sing for us.'

—

We stroll along the empty city streets. It's off-season, Sunday night. Apparently even Rio has to rest occasionally. Along the beach a small kiosk bar emerges from the darkness like a beacon. We order a couple of coconut drinks prepared by the skilful use of a small sabre. We drink them with the dark sea at our feet bordered by white sand, the waves beyond, unseen.

We sip our drinks.

A small thin man carrying a plastic bag appears before us.

The Duke loves to show off his ability to speak at least a little bit of every language in the world. He greets the man with, *'Alo, boa noit.'*

The man speaks quietly in Portuguese. He speaks quickly. He gestures to the plastic bag every so often.

'Sorry, but we don't understand,' says the Duke.

'*Eu sou* confused,' says Edmund.

We all shake our heads and show our palms in mild confusion.

The man stops and looks at us.

'What's in the bag, mate?' tries the Prince.

'Show us,' says Edmund.

We all mime opening something.

The man slowly unties the plastic bag. Inside the bag is a box wrapped in brown paper and string. He painfully loosens the knots. One is caught. It takes a while to unravel. He unfolds the paper. It is a shoebox held together with big rubber bands. He places each rubber band neatly on the ground.

We sip our drinks.

The lid comes off. There is newspaper inside. He puts his hands into the newspaper and takes out a dead pigeon wrapped in a plastic bag. He takes the pigeon from the plastic bag and shows it to us on outstretched hands.

We stare at it mutely.

He takes some seed from his pocket and tries to feed it.

It hangs limply in his hands. Its head lies at a strange angle over his fingers.

He holds the pigeon to his chest. It seems that he loves the pigeon very much.

He indicates that he's going to keep on walking.

We nod and make sorry sounds.

He goes on his way.

We sip our drinks.

In a little while he fades into the far darkness, enveloped in the indifferent night.

'So, *que voce pensa de mim assim distante?*' says the Duke.

'What do you think of me so far?' translates Edmund.

—

It's time to move on. We pass by the sand sculptures. Wonderful structures. Written despite the wind.

'I want to play sandcastles,' squeals the Princess.

She runs down to the beach and begins mashing handfuls of sand onto the side of a finely detailed medieval castle replete with servants milling in the courtyard and a carriage approaching the gate. She crashes through the stables and falls onto a delicately wrought horse.

I can't watch. Edmund and I leave the Duke and the Prince to look after her. We'll get in trouble for that later. We find a stretch of beach and watch the dawn rise over the Atlantic Ocean. Living on the event horizon. The view is great from here.

—

Edmund and I pack up the room, which hasn't been slept in, and meet the Duke in the hall on our way out to grab something to eat before the taxi arrives. The Duke is in a state.

'You won't believe what the Princess did. The Prince and I finally dragged her away from the sandcastles and got her home after the dancing-in-the-waves incident. We put our heads down for a couple of hours because she's so exhausting, as you know, darling, and when we woke up, her bed was in front of the door. During the night she had shifted all the furniture around the room. The beds we were sleeping in had been moved. I woke up in the bathroom. Very disconcerting.'

'Now, don't give me that look,' says the Duke.

I try not to give him that look.

We reach a food stand. Edmund eyes off the coconut pretzels and confidently steps up to the counter. 'A *pretzel de cocó.*'

The girl looks puzzled for a moment.

And then she laughs a little. And then she laughs again. And then it takes a full minute before she can speak. And when she can speak, she calls out to a friend and tells him what Edmund has said. And then he starts laughing.

'What did I say?' asks Edmund.

'You just asked for a pretzel of poo,' says the Duke.

—

Taxi to airport, doze on the plane, grab bags which are, of course, last onto the carousel because we have to make a connection, and we take a taxi though the heart of São Paulo. And what a broken heart she has. The horrorscape of a city on the edge of the world. New desolations rise to meet us on the horizon over and over again but the airport is new and clean.

The others are annoyed we took the holiday and don't seem very interested in our stories. They scowl at us when we're not looking.

The Lady is looking even more gaunt than usual. 'I saved so much money in Brazil,' she says. 'It was impossible to find anything to eat besides rice and beans. It's so hard being a vegetarian in this country. I decided to treat myself with all of the money I saved on some nice perfume.'

The Lady reaches into her bag and produces a large bottle of Chanel. The flagon of scent looks unwieldy in her bony hands. The Lady sprays the perfume into the air and walks through the cloud of fragrance like a 1930s actress. Her expression of feminine bliss slides sideways as she does. She begins to lose consciousness from the heady mix redolent with alcohol and synthesised odorants. I personally think lack of food also has something to do with it. The Prince seems to think so too and steps in just at the crest of the Lady's faint. The Lady rouses herself somewhat at the press of the softly dense muscles of the Prince's arms. As you would, in her position. In those arms.

'Do you want to get something to eat?' asks the Prince good-naturedly.

'Maybe I do,' says the Lady. 'Something light.'

'Like you,' says the Prince as he leads the Lady away. She revives a little more at the blatant flattery and smiles weakly at the Prince.

'Don't forget to count your change,' shouts the Chancellor after them.

'I'm off to look at hand creams,' says the Duke.

When the Duke says 'look' he means cover himself in a protective layer of various moisturisers at Duty Free. He rarely buys anything but always looks nice and moist on a flight.

'Me too,' says the Princess. She takes the Duke's hand in hers like they're going on a date. 'You have baby hands.'

This time, it's the Duke who gives me that look.

Edmund and I decide to do some shopping as well and spend the last of our Reals. We pass the Generalissimo crashed out in the arrivals lounge. His sunglasses are set at a jaunty, Dutch angle on his face. We don't wake him as we walk by.

'What do you think of this T-shirt?' Edmund holds out

a not entirely unpleasant shirt with a picture of Ipanema on it.

'Nice.'

'I'm going to get it.'

'The woman behind the counter probably speaks English. Maybe just ask for it in English this time.'

Edmund is confident. Edmund is upstanding. Edmund raises himself to his full height.

'*Uma camishinha grande com Ipanema*,' he says with more than a hint of pride.

The woman smiles. Not unkindly.

'I'm sorry sir, we don't have any extra large condoms with Ipanema on them at this store.'

Dubai

I was here years ago when Dubai was nothing more than a road leading to a port next to a scrubby tree. It was a time of few cars, when markets were made of timber and energetic voices and not a single man-made island adorned the shore. Now Dubai is made up of seven star hotels, big black Hummers and mega shopping centres in which no one seems to be able to afford to shop. Absurd Dubai with its indoor ski park, fragrant Dubai with its oily perfumes and cruel Dubai with its indentured slaves, the thin men from the Indian subcontinent working on building sites in the middle of the day. These dusty men with their sinewy, efficient bodies making skyscrapers with sand only to return at night to a whole bunk bed they can call their very own. The cranes, all 75 per cent of the world's cranes, litter the horizon. But the desert has remained the same: dry, fragile and indifferent. People couldn't live here in the summer time until air conditioning was invented. Dubai inhales power like I take breath. Without air conditioning, Dubai is simply a lot of tall buildings filled with empty rooms. And a ski park full of water.

We're doing a show for the Very Important People at a corporate event before the Dubai World Cup. The racing of horses is really big around here. And camels. A camel is probably not as graceful as a horse but I can see the fun in racing them.

Around here the men wear white and the women wear black. I guess so they can tell each other apart. Flashes of western clothes and sky-high heels peek from underneath great, black capes. These people, at first sight, seem to be afraid of their own imaginations. But then again, this is the desert. Long coats for the ladies and ostensibly dresses for the gentlemen are judicious here. The sun has no mercy in the desert. Westerners in short shorts and strappy singlets seem to lack a certain common sense in this part of world. Not that the locals seem to mind. Dubai is a tolerant place, on the whole. This is not Saudi Arabia. We never get asked to perform in Saudi Arabia.

Outside the window of the bus, tall buildings made of glass line up and stand to attention as we pass. The Princess decides to give us a commentary.

'Dubai has the tallest outline in the world. One famous building, the Burger Arab, was built to resemble a dhow. A dhow is otherwise known as Chinese junk,' she says.

I look to see what our presenter, Akilah, makes of this statement. She is a very handsome woman in her forties draped in fabric with large, dark brown eyes.

'Yes, Dubai has a rich collection of buildings of various architectural styles. Many modern interpretations of Islamic architecture can be found here,' says Akilah, without missing a beat.

We drive over a large body of water flowing into the sea. 'This is Dubai Creek,' says Akilah. 'We call it Khor Dubai.'

'Where I come from,' says the Prince, 'we'd call that a very wide river.'

'It's not a river. It's salt water,' says Akilah.

'Where does the drinking water come from then?'

'From the creek.'

'You drink salt water?'

'After it's been through the desalination plant.'

'What do you do with the leftover salt?'

'They sprinkle it on their chips,' says the Duke.

'Cool,' says the Prince.

—

We rehearse the show to suit conservative tastes. For this show our love becomes courtly, our excesses toned down and the costumes modified for modesty's sake. We cut out a section of the show we think might be regarded as too risqué. We take out things that might offend and more, just in case. By the end of the rehearsal we have a pleasant show: dull, pretty and utterly inoffensive.

Everyone is lying on the floor of the dressing room. We are warming up; having that quiet conversation you have with your body before a show. Edmund is rolling slowly, his body spiralling into the floor in consecutive sections. The Princess lies with one of her legs beside her head in a rare moment of calm. The Lady is lounging in an extreme stretch that looks like she's trying to switch her legs around. The Prince is helping her. I wonder if I see something almost invisible pass between them. The Generalissimo is winding up rope slowly and methodically in his freakishly oversized hands.

The Duke breaks the calm by bursting through the door and storming over to the Generalissimo.

'I take it your intention is either to kill or cause grievous bodily harm to the members of this company.'

The Generalissimo rolls his eyes. 'What are you talking about?'

'I found loose bolts in the rig. Eight of them. They were a twist of the thread away from falling out completely.'

'I checked all the bolts. They were fine.'

'This can't happen again. Do you understand me? This cannot happen again or I will . . .'

'What?'

The Duke replies by outlining what he proposes to do to the Generalissimo. It doesn't sound as if it would be much fun at all.

The Generalissimo, in response, calls the Duke a very unpleasant name.

'Guys. Language,' says the Lady.

'Very well,' says the Duke. ' I am sick of you not giving a *noun*. You will hurt someone if you continue the way you are going you *adjective, adjective noun. Verb* you!'

'Oh fuck off,' says the Generalissimo and disappears out the door.

—

We play to a very large group of very drunk English expats. These people are tanked, plastered, hammered, steaming, trolleyed, blathered, pished, lashed, snockered, slaughtered, wankered, munted, drunk. One of the ladies actually falls off a low balcony. Legs akimbo, she enables a view of her panties for one and all. In another part of the ground two men are slow dancing with each other and in another section a man looks like he has just wet himself.

The Arabs sit on couches on stages scattered around the grounds and drink tea or nothing. Apparently one of the king's twenty-one children is there but I don't see him. Even if I did know what he looked like.

We didn't need to change the show. We could be doing live sex acts out here and no one would notice.

—

Everyone is on the bus except for Edmund and the Princess. We have been waiting now for about an hour. An hour. Edmund finally comes into view, strolling along.

'He could at least pretend he gives a damn,' says the Duke.

Edmund appears at the front of the bus. He recoils a little at the sight of so many scowling faces.

'What?' says Edmund.

'Where have you been?' asks the Duke in a barely controlled voice.

'I lost my wallet.'

'Did you find it?'

'In the end.'

'And where was it?'

'In my pants.'

The Duke takes a deep breath. 'Have you seen the Princess?'

'She not here yet?'

'When was the last time you saw her?'

'She was talking to an English guy at the party.'

'Sit down,' says the Duke.

Edmund sits down.

Akilah runs up to the bus. 'Your friend has been arrested,' she says.

'Arrested? What for?' The Duke is aghast.

'They are talking about arresting her for offending public decency.'

'What was she doing?' asks Edmund.

'She was found having sex in a public place.'

The Duke's horror is as animated as a silent movie star. 'Okay, okay, okay, you all go back to the hotel and I'll come with you, Akilah.'

He bounds out the door like a rabbit after her billowing black cape. The bus pulls away into the night.

———

At breakfast the Duke takes a sip of his tea. 'So the policeman said he was walking around the course when a couple of guys stopped him and said that there was a man having sex with a woman on the racetrack. He took his torch and found them. Apparently at first he just asked them to stop but when he came back 10 minutes later they were still at it. The Princess says they were just hugging and kissing. And that she didn't insult Islam and abuse the officer when he arrested her.'

'What's going to happen to her?' asks the Lady, breathless with anticipation.

'Akilah did something possibly illegal and somehow convinced the officer to let the incident go if the Princess was put on the first available flight out of town. Her flight would have left by now.'

Everyone leans back on his or her chair. Yet again the Princess has left us all speechless.

The Chancellor pipes up. 'Pick up for the airport is 8 am tomorrow. You all have the rest of the day off.'

I realise the Chancellor's been keeping a low profile through all of this.

'But I'm off now,' says the Duke. 'I have to go via London. The Office needs me to sort something out. I'll see you in Mumbai.'

—

Edmund, the Prince, the Lady and I spend the day shopping. We become dizzy from the scents and shiny surfaces and escalators going in every direction. I wonder if Escher wasn't predicting the future of architecture after all.

Edmund disappears up an escalator where the normal laws of gravity don't seem to apply while the rest of us stop for coffee so expensive that I wonder if I shouldn't have just had water and kept the price of the coffee for a deposit on a small house. He reappears with shopping bags.

'What did you buy?' I ask him when he joins us at the table.

'I bought some guthras and a matching egal,' says Edmund.

'Once more in English?' asks the Lady.

Edmund reaches into his bags and produces a red and white headscarf as worn by the UAE men around Dubai. 'This is a guthra.' Edmund then produces a length of black rope fashioned into a circle with long bits of rope dangling from the end. 'And this is an egal. The egal keeps the guthra in place.' Edmund tries the headdress on. It doesn't look like the way the local men wear it. He looks like a young girl with big ears and a tablecloth on her head.

'That looks great, Edmund,' I say. 'You should have bought two.'

'I did,' says Edmund, as he brings another guthra from his bag. 'I bought a white one for summer and a black one for formal occasions.'

I doubt he'll ever have a black guthra event to go to but I don't mention it.

After dinner at an Indian place we can afford we find ourselves back at the hotel bar. A waiter in a well-pressed shirt and manners approaches us to take our order. Edmund peruses the wine list.

'We'll get one large bottle to share.'

'Will that be enough?' asks the Prince.

'Two large bottles to share,' says Edmund.

'How many glasses are in a bottle?'

'Two glasses,' I say.

'How about three?' says the Lady.

'Four, four bottles to share,' says Edmund. 'Is that enough?'

'I hope so,' says the Prince.

After four bottles to share the Prince suggests we go to the rooftop pool for a swim. This sounds like a great idea after four bottles to share. We hurry off to our rooms for our togs and agree to meet at the pool.

The doors of the lift open and there is the Lady.

'It's closed,' she says.

'Probably should have checked the opening times before we got changed,' I say.

The Prince appears from around a corner. 'I've found another way in,' he says.

We can hear a conversation around another corner. I hear his voice before I see him. It's low, so low it is almost beyond perception. I sense the vibrations and then Edmund appears with a man I have never seen before.

'This is a friend of mine from college. I found him in the lift. He's staying here as well.'

'I'm Hardi Hamid,' says the man in his dulcet tones.

'Harmi Hardi?'

'No Hardi Hamid.' And he hangs out in the ah sounds for a while.

Particles act like waves. Waves like particles. I can hear the paradox. The very quality of the universe from his mouth. It's a nice mouth.

'Follow me,' says the Prince, and disappears through a door.

We follow the Prince up a flight of stairs to the roof. The pool beckons on the other side of a very tall wire fence.

'You game?' asks the Prince with the cheeky smile.

I'm not so sure. 'Maybe we should stop breaking rules in this country and just go back to the bar.'

'Chicken.'

'Calling me a tasty, flightless bird is not going to compel me to do what you say.'

'Fine,' says the Prince. He jumps up on the fence.

Besides the unhappy prospect of breaking another law in a foreign country, the other thing that makes me hesitate is the part of the climb that involves a moment when you have to be, technically, on the outside of the building with only the ground twenty floors beneath you. Seems a lot of effort for a quick swim. I probably won't even put my head under.

The Lady and Edmund don't seem to care about this precarious part of the climb and follow the Prince up without a word.

Hardi Hamid offers his hand in the manner of a gentleman. 'Will you be joining us?'

I don't take his hand but haul myself up the wire structure. He follows after me. I wish that he wasn't looking at me from that angle. I should have let him go first. I mean, I've just met him.

We are mindful of our subterfuge and move silently around the banana lounges. Five lithe bodies slip into the still and cosy water. The pool is a dark oasis softened by the brilliant moon and the water is as warm as a cup of tea with milk. The firmament envelops us in its magnificent indifference.

Edmund breaks the reverie. 'I'm going back to the bar. Who's coming?'

'Maybe one more cheeky one,' says the Prince.

'Let's go,' says the Lady.

'Stay a little longer?' says Hardi Hamid in a voice that feels like an act of telepathy. 'We can follow the others down in a minute.'

'We'll follow you down in a minute,' I say without hesitation and try not to see if any looks are exchanged between my fellows. The others leave and negotiate the fence as casually as if it was a door.

We glide to the shallows and drift in the water illuminated in that old flatterer, the moon. Hardi Hamid tells me a story in velvet tones while we gently move through the dark water.

'There was an old farmer whose horse ran away one day. His neighbours said, "What awful luck." The old farmer said, "Maybe 'tis, maybe 'tisn't." The following morning the horse returned, bringing with it three other wild horses. "How wonderful," said the neighbours. "Maybe 'tis, maybe 'tisn't," said the old farmer. The next day the old farmer's son tried to ride one of the wild horses but he was thrown and broke his leg. "Such bad luck," said the neighbours. "Maybe 'tis, maybe 'tisn't," said the old farmer. The following day military officials came to the village to draft young men into the army. Since the son had a broken leg, the military officials passed him by. The neighbours congratulated the old farmer on how well things had turned out. "Maybe 'tis, maybe 'tisn't," said the old farmer.'

When Hardi Harmid asks me to come with him I don't say maybe, I say, 'As long as it's somewhere private.'

I try not to wake him when I leave. He looks like Endymion in repose. I slip quietly out the door. It closes with a small click. I turn around and down the hall Edmund is doing exactly the same thing. Behind him the Prince is leaving another room. With tacit under-standing we all creep towards the lift. Edmund even has his shoes in his hand. The elevator arrives and we file in. The doors close smoothly behind us.

In the lift the piped music plays the call to prayer.

Bombay

We are coming in low over the slums. So low I feel like I can almost make out the faces of the great roiling masses walking between flat-roofed rooms subdivided by narrow streets. Technicolor India. I slip a coffee spoon into my pocket. I'm pleased with my spoon. First one from Air India.

Indians are at lots of airports around the world so at first it doesn't feel like we've necessarily landed in India. When we emerge from customs I get a flash of Rio. Must be the palm trees. A young boy and a girl thereafter gesture to us for money, money for food. Hand to mouth, they gesture, hand to mouth.

On the bus to our hotel, the city unfolds. Poverty crowds around us. Colourful poverty but single tent living never ceases to confront. Traffic is an interminable rumbling punctuated by horns and people living in the dirt by the roadside cooking and talking and pissing and sleeping. Rooms without roofs constructed with only simple modesty walls made of cloth and cardboard boxes. The sellers wander the streets with fruit and all I can see is sickness in a basket for a soft westerner like me. A woman rides side-saddle on the back of a motorbike. She's asleep, without a helmet and her only security is a hand she has tucked into the driver's pocket.

Gradually the streets get cleaner, the shops more western and we know we must be nearing our hotel. We've all stopped taking photographs and just gaze out of the window and some of us have stopped doing even that. It's a long trip.

When we pull up at the hotel we are greeted by men in gold-trimmed turbans and fancy red coats. They insist on doing everything for us: open doors, carry luggage, hand us chilled drinks. I wonder what would happen if I asked one of them for a quick shoulder massage. They look like they might oblige.

The Chancellor once more puts out the call and demands that we all hand her our passports. In the stampede to the desk everyone begins the plaintive call, 'A corner room? Can I have a corner room away from the lift?'

'Do they have smoking rooms?'

'I want one with a balcony.'

The Princess is already at the hotel. She's been waiting for a couple of hours. She looks bored, tired and even more bonkers than usual. She looks like Giselle in the final act. She is the first to be assigned her room. The man in the turban looks prepared to carry her to her accommodation. She disappears into the lift with a haughty air.

My room is fine. It is a quirky two-level corner apartment with mirrors on the ceilings. Fancy. And a touch disturbing. There is a knock at the door. The Princess sweeps into my room.

'Your room is much better.' She walks around it like a real estate agent. She smiles. It's not a pretty smile.

'You have to change rooms with me.'

'No I don't.'

'But you have to. I need space to do my hula-hoops.'

The Princess, to my horror, has brought hula-hoops.

'Ask the people at the front desk to change your room. They seem very accommodating.'

'I want this room. It's bigger and you can see the bay from here.'

'I am under no obligation to change rooms with you.'

'Change with me.'

'Nothing could compel me to change with you.'

'Change with me.'

'No.'

'CHANGE WITH ME!'

'Please leave my room.'

'No.'

The Princess sits on the floor.

'Please leave my room.'

'No, I will not.' The Princess shakes her head.

I start to unpack my bag. She sits defiant. I finish unpacking my bag. She sits defiant. I lie on the bed. She sits ever defiant. I turn on the television, make a cup of tea, finish my cup of tea and then I sit on the edge of the bed. I look at the Princess. I prepare for actual violence. The Princess and I engage in a staring competition. I drain all signs of compassion from my face. She blinks.

'Leave my room,' I say very, very quietly.

The Princess glares at me with the rage of a psychotic child, stamps her foot and makes her grand exit, making sure to knock over a lamp on the way.

—

As I walk through the foyer to go to dinner the Princess

emerges from a lift accompanied by an attendant who is carrying her bags with the look of the long suffering.

'No, I don't want that room either,' she declares to the busy foyer. 'The position of the bathroom does not suit me.'

—

The first meal in India is pizza. The first meal in a new country is usually exactly the wrong choice and you always pay too much. Although still unwashed after two days on a plane, we finally begin to land.

Edmund fancies himself as a bit of a comedian.

'Hey guys, I've got a new light bulb joke I want to tell you.'

'Must you?' sighs the Chancellor.

'How many Freudians does it take to change a light bulb?' He smiles expectantly at the group. 'Two. One to change the light bulb and one to hold the penis, I mean, ladder.'

The Prince decides to join in. 'How many actors does it take to change a light bulb? One. The actor holds the light bulb while the rest of the world revolves around him.'

'I have a joke,' says the Chancellor.

The Chancellor is going to tell a joke? We turn to her in surprise.

'What? I tell jokes,' she says.

'Well, go on then,' encourages Edmund.

'Knock, knock?'

'Who's there?' asks Edmund.

'Madam.'

'Madam who?'

'M'damn fist's stuck in the door.'

The Chancellor told a joke.

I get to my feet. 'I'm off to have a shower. Anyone want to meet in the foyer in an hour for a walk?'

'Yeah, I'll come for a walk,' says Edmund.

'Me too,' says the Lady.

No one else is interested.

'See you in an hour then,' I say, and throw some money on the table.

'I have another one,' says Edmund as I walk away. 'How many philosophers does it take to change a light bulb? Define "light bulb".'

—

Outside the restaurant a man is selling books on the side of the road. I find a copy of *The Karma Sutra*. I hold the book out.

'How much for this?'

'One thousand rupees,' he replies efficiently.

I feel obliged to barter. I hate to barter. It turns shopping into a blood sport. I move as if to walk away, saying over my shoulder, 'Five hundred rupees.'

He's having none of it.

'Madam,' he patiently explains, 'you are an educated, western woman while I am a bookseller who cannot read. One thousand rupees.'

Now I have to buy the damn book.

An old cow ambles past and I realise I have never seen an old cow before. I feel guilty. I realise that where I come from, cows never achieve old age. They reach my plate long before they reach their dotage.

A tiny old woman puts her hand on me.

'No money. I have no money. Go away. Let me go,' I say but I've dropped the key to my hotel room and she's returning it. I am humbled. I am sorry. I give her money. This is India. Everything is not as it seems.

—

The Lady, Edmund and I meet back in the foyer after we've freshened up in our rooms with the mirrors on the ceiling. Edmund wonders if he didn't see a bald spot on his head in one of the overhead reflections. The Lady and I assure him that he is definitely going prematurely bald. He can't see the funny side. We laugh at him anyway. The night is warm as we pick our way among the stalls and through the families living on rugs.

A young girl finds the Lady. The girl wears a bright sari, a gold stud in her nose and a long plait, which snakes along her spine. The Lady is entranced. She's brought her camera on the walk. She points it at the girl.

'Beautiful girl, aren't you? You're very beautiful.'

The girl makes a face.

'She's very beautiful,' says the Lady to me.

The girl looks at the ground.

'Nice,' says the girl, mostly to herself. The Lady looks at the girl through her camera.

'WHAT . . . IS . . . YOUR . . . NAME?' asks the Lady.

'Mandy.'

'Melvin?'

The girl looks confused.

'And how old are you, Melvin?' continues the Lady.

'Ten.'

'And what do you want to be when you grow up?'

'Oh . . . I . . . my brother, one.'

'One year old?'

'Yes. No walking.'

'What?'

'No walking.'

'And what's your job?'

'Job here.' Mandy gestures to the street.

'And what's that?'

'What?'

'You speak English very well.'

'Thank you.'

'You're very smart, Melvin. Think so?'

Mandy reaches for the Lady's camera.

'Show me.'

The Lady hesitates but then hands over the equipment. Mandy looks at it carefully and makes a sly comment in a language I've never heard before to some onlookers standing nearby. And then she takes a photograph of the Lady. The flash briefly illuminates the Lady's surprised face. And then Mandy hands the camera back with a broad smile.

A man in a turban magically appears at my elbow in just the way you would expect a man in a turban would appear.

'*Namaste.*'

'Hello.'

'I absolutely must read your palm. I insist,' he insists.

'But I don't want my palm read.'

'I can tell you are a spiritual person.'

'No I'm not.'

He has my hand. 'Yes you are.'

'I'm not.'

'You are.'

We disagree with each other for a while.

'Listen, when I hear the word "spiritual" I reach for my gun. And I really don't want to know my future,' I say, to break the impasse. He's still holding my hand. His hand is soft and larger than my own. If he holds it much longer he'll have to buy me dinner.

'You will marry late.'

'No kidding.'

'You will be comfortable in your old age,' he says, still holding my hand.

'Glad to hear it.'

'You need to enjoy the journey more than you do.'

'Okay,' I say and take back my hand.

Edmund, listening into the conversation, has a question for the man in the turban.

'What does *namaste* mean?'

'So,' says the man in the turban, 'you have no real control over the birth and the death. You can postpone death a bit, you really can't control your birth, so what you can essentially manage is the journey between birth and death. So, birth is one extreme, death is the other opposite. The journey, the life, the journey is, the *namaste*.' And he holds his hands as if ready to pray and moves them through the arc, signifying each state. 'Do not cling to anything. That is what the Indian yoga tradition and spiritual tradition is. Do not get yourself attached to any material or any such things because that will inevitably bring you disappointment.' He brings his palms together. 'So therefore, do not cling.'

I give the man in the turban some money and he goes away.

—

We come across a dark, young woman with wide eyes holding a baby in her arms. The Lady reaches out to touch the baby's cheek. The dark, young woman looks nervously at Mandy. Mandy moves swiftly between the Lady and the baby.

'No. She is from bad family.' Mandy pulls the Lady away. The dark, young woman looks at me with the widest eyes. Her eyes are more than a little frightened. She pulls the baby a little closer to herself. I give her some money and I go away.

———

I find Edmund trying on one of those big white shirts that men wear in India. It's so long it touches the ground.

'What do you think?' he asks me.

'You look great. You've got to get it. I'd get two if I were you.'

'You know what? I will.' And he preens a little in the mirror.

The Lady appears. Mandy is nowhere to be seen.

'Where's your little friend? I thought you'd started the adoption process,' I say.

The Lady winces a little. 'She wanted me to buy rice, oil and formula for her baby brother so we found a shop and I bought rice, oil and formula for her baby brother and then I couldn't find her again.'

'So, you gave her some money and she went away.'

'Quite a lot of money actually,' and the Lady looks pained.

'How much?'

The Lady tells us how much.

'My goodness, that is a lot.' I can't help but gasp a little.

'Oh well, it's only money.'

The Lady tries to look as if she doesn't mind.

—

The Duke has arrived on a later flight. He's come in from London. We meet at the hotel bar. A guy plays 'Up Where We Belong' on an organ in the corner and all the waiters have impeccable manners.

The Duke looks fit and he's funny and all is well in the world as we exuberantly order another drink.

He greets me with, 'Darling, so good to see you. You look tremendous.'

'As do you.'

'The Office is very happy with our extremely fine performances eliciting a wonderful response all over Brazil. As for Dubai, the Office hears that it was a seamless gig.'

'Glad to hear the Office is happy,' I say, and I am.

'I've just come from England where I caught up with the lover,' continues the Duke. 'We've moved into a seventeen-room Victorian manor with a conservatory the size of Texas.'

'Sounds awful, darling,' I say. 'And how is the lover?'

'Ivan? Oh my god. Who knew?'

Ivan's the new boyfriend.

'He's a brilliant artist,' he says. 'Extremely smart, speaks with an outrageously sexy accent, half my age and he wants, wants, wants me. He loves me in various ways and we can wander the streets together with no hope of destination just laughing and loving and eating and drinking and smoking. So of course, I just feel lovely.'

'Oh how the gods smile when they smile,' I say.

'I do love London but the British can be a funny lot.

I mean, why do the English get so excited about the prospect of a hot beverage? Or why is it that when they are finally at the cash register after those interminable queues, they seem surprised that they are being asked for money at all and go "Oh" in such a surprised way, as if they have never been asked for money before and spend five minutes searching through their purses as if the pound was a foreign currency?'

He takes a sip of his drink.

'Oh God,' says the Duke, suddenly serious, 'I hope we get all the gear tomorrow. The freight's stuck at customs and I've been calling all day going . . .' At this point he breaks into gibberish, miming phone calls. The table helpfully breaks into gibberish with him. We play the guys at customs on the other end of the phone. We all try to be as unhelpful as possible. The Duke's dumb show gets increasingly more frantic. It finishes with him weeping into his pretend phone. He returns to speaking English again.

'The thing is, I can't be stressed by this. The gear is supposed to be arriving at one. I said three to the guy and he said how about four, four-thirty, which in this country means the following day. It might not get here in time. We might have to rehearse late. But it's going to be a beautiful show when the gear does arrive. The site is great.'

The site is indeed great. We are performing in front of the Gateway of India, the waiting room for the British at the height of their colonial powers. A very majestic, very imposing waiting room. Ironically, the Gateway was never used for any triumphal receptions for English royalty but stood instead as a mute sentinel to the dawn of Indian independence as the last of the Commonwealth troops in India left from its soaring arches. Now it's fenced off so no one can use it. The people wait for boats crowded around, but not underneath, its grand arches, legs hanging along the stone wall of the harbour.

'So who's doing the extra shows?' asks the Princess.

'Haven't you got the notes?' asks the Duke.

'No I don't have anything.' The Princess looks very concerned.

'No notes?' The Duke returns her concerned face.

'No notes.'

The Duke looks at Edmund. 'Did you get notes?'

'No, no notes.'

The Duke looks around the table. 'I was waiting for the Office to make the difficult decisions.'

The Duke realises he has to do the dirty work. He balances delicately on the tightrope of people's feelings.

'Yeah . . . no . . . I know . . . I'd feel the same way in your position . . . no, they didn't give a reason . . . no, I don't know why . . . yeah . . . no . . . yeah . . . no . . . I know.'

The Duke, keen for a distraction now all the disappointments have been dispensed, changes the subject.

'I'm seventy-five kilograms,' he suddenly announces to the table.

'You look just the same,' I say. He does.

'No, I'll show you.' He lifts his shirt then pretends to sob.

'I'm sixty-nine,' says Edmund.

'I'm forty-one,' says the Lady.

The table breaks into a cacophony of numbers about everyone's current weight and implications with regards to equipment. A secret language between us.

'Have I got 109?' asks Edmund.

'No, you have 43,' says the Duke.

'I don't want 43, it has a bias.'

'It does,' agrees the Prince. 'I used it in Brazil and had a terrible time of it.'

'Did the Office pack 61?' asks the Lady.

'I think I saw 61 go in with the freight,' says the Duke.

'New clamps?' asks Edmund.

'Half and half,' replies the Duke.

'Of course you have 102 for me,' says the Princess.

'No, you have 101.'

'But I always use 102,' says the Princess, as if speaking to a young child.

'You can't use 102 because it isn't here.'

'But I want to use 102.'

I can't bear to listen to this so I loudly order another round. The Duke is trapped in one of the Princess's circles of hell. The drinks arrive and the Duke, by leading a toast, narrowly distracts the Princess. We raise our glasses to each other and our new adventure. We all meet each other's eyes with each chink of the glass. The Duke places his wine upon the table and looks all pleased.

'I'm going to Haridwar.'

He deliberately mispronounces it as Hardware and everyone enjoys saying Hardware for a bit. Now everyone's going to Hardware.

'I'm going to meditate up the Ganges,' says the Duke. 'I might levitate all the way.' He purrs like an air hostess. 'If you look to your left you will see the Clock Tower and if you look to your right you will see Vishnu. I'm going to visit all the temples. Become an ashram.'

'Become an ashram?' The Lady is confused.

'Well you know my body is a farm. No really, seriously. My body's been an ashram for so many years now. Oh honey, if you only knew. Ashram with a carport, a railway station and its own airport.'

Ten-second answers

We have a media call. Our make-up is immaculate. We have lost our identities in our pretend faces. We are framed by the Gateway of India. Myriad cameras greet us and the urgency of the Indian journalists press upon us.

You must remember certain things when dealing with the media. First of all, perception is believing and I'm not talking about the truth. Be receptive to the press. Welcome them into your lounge room smiling and on the balls of your feet. Say g'day to everyone. Be thrilled. DUA: Don't Use Acronyms. Key messages. Ten-second answers. Have an answer to every question. Especially, 'Why don't you get a real job?' Be noticed. Be remembered. Be credible. Be preferred. Ask the photographer, 'Will it be a head and shoulders?' Then put your hands behind your back.

The questions come in quick succession. Nothing we haven't answered before.

'Yes, it's fun.'

'No, I'm sorry, you can't have a go.'

'No, I'm not afraid of heights.'

'Oh, yes, it's perfectly safe.'

The Prince does a handstand for the media. It goes down well.

—

I'm pulled aside to do a radio interview over the phone. Two hyperactive voices, a man and a woman, cheerfully yell at me down the line. They speak Hindi and English, at what seems the very same time. They demand that I say *namaste* for *Good Morning Mumbai* and then break into manic laughter.

I have no choice but to comply.

'*Namaste*, Mumbai.'

I do my best to sound extremely enthusiastic.

Now they manage to laugh and speak at the very same time. '*Namaste* Mumbai,' they parrot back, '*Namaste* Mumbai.' I'm not too sure what's going on but they seem to be having lots of fun. Suddenly it's goodbye from them and it's goodbye from me but the line goes dead before I can get the words out.

All the photos have been taken, all the names spelt out for the print media and it's time to go. We smile and wave and begin to make our way back to the dressing rooms.

The Princess hangs back. She begins bowing like a Prima Ballerina. Slowly, gracefully from side to side taking in an enormous audience that isn't there. The reporters look sideways at each other and start to pack up their cameras. She continues her curtsying and bowing with increasingly exaggerated flourishes. She is humble. She is magnanimous. She is stark raving mad. The press start to walk away. She prostrates herself on the ground as the dying swan. The Duke walks over to her, speaking gently.

'Come on, Princess. Show's over. Time to go.'

The Princess looks at him without seeing. 'Time to . . . go?'

'Here, take my hand.'

'But my audience loves me, needs me.' She is suddenly a very earnest, very young child.

'Come on Princess. This way.'

She takes the Duke's hand. She staggers to her feet. She's left the building. With infinite gentleness, he leads her away. She smiles her crazy fixed smile at the media that have long gone. She begins murmuring to herself. 'But my audience, my audience love me, need me.'

'We need you too,' the Duke says as he puts an arm around her shoulders.

—

The Gateway of India looms impressively behind us as we prepare to run the show. We're here to rehearse. It's protocol. Try out the new site, check the equipment and freshen up the routines. Tensions tend to come to the surface during rehearsals. I tread carefully. You never know who's going to be up to their knees in trouble before they notice the danger. Getting on the wrong side of someone in this company can be like walking into quicksand: impossible to back out of before you are swallowed in the mire. We get through the run and descend for notes from the Duke.

As we stretch on the ground, a crowd of onlookers with apparently nowhere else to be just now surrounds us.

'Edmund, you missed the cue at the beginning of the second act,' begins the Duke.

'But the Princess didn't give me the nod. I thought I had to wait for the nod.'

'I nodded at you.' The Princess seems very sure about this.

'No you didn't.'

'Yes I did. I almost nodded my head off.'

'You did not.'

'I did.'

'Did not.'

'DID!'

The Duke has to intervene.

'Whatever, just remember for the show, okay?'

'Fine.'

The Princess nods at Edmund. The onlookers nod along helpfully behind them.

'Right,' the Duke puts an end to the nodding crowd with his own nod. 'Lady, I'd like to see you make your entrance like a queen. With the dignity of a queen. Think Queen Elizabeth.'

Before the Lady can answer, the Princess pipes up.

'Queen Elizabeth the First was the virgin queen. They used to call her Gloria.'

'That's very good, Princess . . .'

'Around the same time Sir Frances Drake circumcised the world with a 100-foot clipper.'

Edmund stifles a laugh. The crowd of onlookers don't. They titter among themselves. The Princess doesn't notice but instead continues with enthusiasm.

'I love Shakespeare although do you know he used to wear women's clothes in the theatre?'

The Duke is getting annoyed now. 'Princess . . .'

'He used to write in Islamic Pentacle so you can never understand what he's saying.'

'We must get on now,' says the Duke.

The Princess leaps into the centre of the group.

'Come, you spirits

That tend on mortal thoughts, unsex me here,

And fill me from the crown to the toe top-full
Of direst cruelty!
With a-hey-nonny, hey-nonny, hey-nonny-nooooooo,'
sings the Princess with a little skipping dance.

'Would you shut up?' This comes from the Lady. Quite out of character. The crowd turns to look at her. The drama of conflict. It's intoxicating.

'You shut up,' says the Princess. The crowd turns back to the Lady.

'No, you shut up,' says the Lady, with ice in her voice.

'Thou shut up thou impertinent, flap-mouthed canker-blossom,' says the Princess.

'Shut up.'

'Thou shut up thou mewling, fat-kidneyed whey face.'

'Shut up.'

'Thou shut up thou beslubbering, beetle-headed bum-bailey.'

The crowd looks like they're watching a tennis match, only these girls are serving insults to each other.

'Why won't you shut up?' says the Lady, the very picture of exasperation.

'Shut up, shut up, shut up, shut up, shut up,' says the Princess, her hands over her ears.

'YOU ARE OUT OF YOUR MIND!'

And then the Princess hits her. Just like that. No warning. Not a slap, not a push but a punch. The Lady goes flying and bleeding onto the ground.

The onlookers go 'Oh!' and surprise turns everyone to stone for a moment.

The Princess shakes out her hand like she's hurt it.

The Lady raises her face. 'Don't hit me,' she says uselessly. Then she looks at her hands, sees the blood falling like rain onto her palms and the tears follow. The Duke appears by her side. He puts his hand on the Lady's back.

'It's all right,' he says, even though it's not. He addresses the group. The onlookers move slightly forward. He is very serious. 'Take a break, everyone.'

Incredibly, the Princess continues, rubbing her hands. 'Out, damned spot! Out, I say! One; two: why, then, 'tis time to do't. Hell is murky!'

'Princess.'

'Fie, my lord, fie! a soldier, and afeard? What need we fear who knows it, when none can call our power to account?'

'Princess.'

'Yet who would have thought the old man to have had so much blood in him?'

'PRINCESS!'

The Duke has spoken. The crowd steps back nervously.

Deeply shocked, we file away. The Princess's eyes meet mine.

'What?' she says, making a stupid face.

I have no answer. I turn my back on her and walk away. This is the point of the tour where I suddenly feel very sure that I've left the iron on at home.

The Wish Goddess

I accompany the Duke to see the Wish Goddess. India has many deities and this one's local and grants wishes from a nearby hill. We bring the Lady along with her black eye. It shows through the heavy make-up. She looks like she walked into a door with a fist in it. We try to be terribly cheerful with her while she says things like 'I didn't deserve that' (of course she didn't), 'I hate her' (so do we) and 'Can you see my black eye?' (of course we can but we don't say so).

We pass by roadside stalls selling juice and suddenly there is the Princess. She is standing in the street sipping unwashed vegetables through a giant straw in the shade of a gigantic cocktail umbrella sticking out of the top of her drink. She smiles broadly in our direction.

An Indian woman flashes past me, and in that instant says, 'Your friend will get very sick drinking that,' and keeps on walking. The Princess continues to stand there and smile at us looking very much like a cautionary advertisement for dumb westerners abroad. Fortunately, the Lady doesn't see her as the Duke and I hurry her away.

After a mostly pleasant walk though the chaotic streets, we reach the Temple of the Wish Goddess.

We are compelled to buy the obligatory offerings of coconuts, bindis and colourful ribbon. We begin to climb the long stairs up to the Wish Goddess.

About halfway up we pass the Chancellor coming down the stairway on a chair. Now, the Chancellor is a woman of some size. Four skinny little guys are carrying her down the stairway on a chair. The skinny little guys are working very hard and sweating profusely. I can't help but feel sorry for the skinny little guys. The Chancellor's generous proportions are exaggerated here. At least she has the decency to look embarrassed about it all. I privately vow never to let someone carry me in a foreign country. Or any country for that matter. We wave and smile at each other but none of us mean it.

At the top of the stairway there are stalls selling perfume and trinkets outside the temple. I can't resist buying something. None of us can. We haven't even gone in and I have perfume oils, the Lady has a questionably loud patterned shawl and the Duke has a mechanical altar comprising pilgrims with movable arms forever reaching to a nameless deity accompanied by a small tune. It is pretty awful. The Lady and I admire it anyway.

We proceed into the temple, which is a cross between a place of worship and a supermarket. The relationship between religion and commerce is very honest here.

We pass by various lesser gods who all need money. These are deities who give change. After you hand over your money, you get your blessing in the form of a dot on your head. By the time I have been blessed, dotted, given bits of string to tie to posts and paid the various deities their cut, I'm not too sure which one was the Wish Goddess. It felt like a great big deity fun park.

I put my shoes back on and find myself completely unmoved. But, still, I made a wish.

'What did you wish for?' asks the Duke.

'Peace on earth.'

'You did not.'

'You're right, I didn't. What did you wish for?'

'Peace on Earth.'

'You did not.'

'You're right.'

'Well, how about you, Lady?' says the Duke. 'What did you wish for?'

Her face is a dark cloud. We walk in silence for a while. It's been a vicious week.

———

The Princess and the Lady carefully avoid each other during the warm-up. In one corner of the room the Princess is spinning her hula-hoops.

'I'm trying to get a four-hoop separation,' says the Princess as her body tries to think of four things at once. A four-hoop separation is when you can keep four hoops circling your body at the same time: one at the neck, one at the chest, one at the waist and one at the knees. The Princess looks like she's having a standing fit.

'Yeah, good luck with that,' I say as the hoops clatter to the ground once more.

I make my way over to the mirrors. I take a seat beside the Duke.

'Hello darling,' he smiles into the mirror. 'How are you travelling tonight?'

'The travelling I like, some of the company not so much.'

'I know the Princess is a bore but what does not kill us and all that.'

One of the hula-hoops flies across the room and hits me in the head.

'Sorry,' yells the Princess and skips over like a little girl to recover the hoop.

I make plans for the hula-hoops.

———

We ascend for the show. The Princess and the Lady are frosty but precise. Now I'm the one missing all the nods. I do everything right, right after everyone else does it. The audience doesn't notice and that's what matters. But the Duke will notice. I miss another nod and then it happens. The Princesses fulfils the prophecy of the passing woman and throws up the roadside juice in a great fetid rainbow above the crowd. A cry of dismay can be heard from the audience. She wipes her mouth, commits to a total state of denial and cues the next move with a nod. Show must go on and all that. And the show does go on, for a crowd that likes us a little less than they did a moment ago.

There is an informal gathering by the truck after the show sans the Princess.

'If she was sick, she shouldn't have gone up. We could have worked it out,' hisses the Lady.

'Some of it hit me,' says Edmund.

'Are you going to tell the office?' asks the Lady, and all eyes turn to the Duke.

'I'll have to put it in the show report. It happened during a show,' he says in his reasonable voice.

'Here she comes,' says the Prince.

'Where are we going for dinner?' asks the Princess as she approaches the group.

'I saw a nice looking place around the corner,' says the Prince. 'Looks like they even have beer.'

'That sounds good,' says the Duke. 'A lovely treat in sober old India.'

Everyone ambles off to dinner. I loiter by the truck getting the rest of my gear together and then I notice the Princess has forgotten to put her hula-hoops in with the rest of the gear. I hesitate for a moment but then I close and lock the back of the truck, wave to the driver and watch the truck move slowly away. I hope the hula-hoops will have a lovely second life with some nice children. A second life far away from me. I sprint to the restaurant to run off some of the guilt I already feel.

The Duke, as usual, doesn't miss much.

'Where have you been?'

'Fans. You know. Kept me talking. Have we ordered yet?'

Agra

Luxurious breakfast. Developing countries always have the best breakfasts. And also England, for some reason. The Duke's late but I don't mind.

'What time did the others get up?' he asks, looking refreshed from his sleep in.

I don't bother to hide my smirk. 'Five-thirty.'

'And in the car?'

'The Chancellor, The Prince, Edmund and the Lady. The Princess is nowhere to be seen and the Generalissimo's smoking hash in his room.'

'I'm so glad we're taking the train. Lets catch a tuk tuk to the station.'

—

And so we catch a tuk tuk to the station. It's a motorbike rickshaw and it's heaps of fun. We haven't really planned this much at all. See how we go travelling blind through New Delhi. We're going to the Taj Mahal today.

—

We make it to the platform just in time to watch the train pull away from the station. We buy tickets for the next one. Fifty-six rupees only. The exchange rate makes that to be about ten cents. The others paid thousands of rupees for their car. We delight at our cleverness, take a two-hour lunch and, at last, the train pulls up to the station.

We find First Class. Air-conditioned, sparsely populated and the catering is good. Unfortunately the conductors realise our mistake all too quickly.

Apparently we have bought Unreserved Second Class Seats. Our task, to find the Unreserved Second Class Seats. We set off.

We find Luggage Class easily enough. Suitcases and boxes and people sitting between the carriages. We hope to each other that these aren't the Unreserved Second Class seats.

The next carriage has seats but so many people are crammed into the moving room they are hanging out the doors. Must be Overcrowded Class. We move on, shimmying between the people.

Now we find ourselves in Walking Up and Down the Train Class, eventually descend into Hold Onto the Open Doorway Class and finally land in Crouching Under the Basin Class. Thankfully we never sink into the horror of Latrine Class.

A man and his wife feel sorry, make some room and offer a seat to me. I look over to the Duke. He's happy flirting with a dangerous looking young man in Open Doorway Class. He won't mind if I take it.

Outside an almost stone-age civilisation is being framed by the moving window. Rice paddies, brickworks and people walking in long, colourful scarves from nowhere to nowhere. When there aren't enough houses for the people to live in, small suburbs made up of tents spring up between the houses. Young boys play cricket in big fields of dirt. They use sticks for bats and pinecones for balls. I figure cricket's popular in India because no one has the energy to play a sport that requires too much running around.

A young boy appears. Mum and Dad have been sitting to my left along the window. He's sick, he's starving and he's dying of something, dying faster than the rest of us. He's so weak he can barely climb the ladder to the bunk above our heads. The way he looks at me tells me that he has already lost interest in life. His mother encourages him and his father guides him up the ladder.

Beggars drag themselves along the floor with mis-shapen limbs and hands with stunted thumbs and forefingers useful only for grasping coins. Boys sweep the carriage floors with their heads down asking for money for a dirty service and always the call of the tea guys, 'Chai, Chai-i!' in resonant voices. The Duke gives one of the Sweepers a lot of money. They lock eyes for a moment. Some understanding passes between them that I don't quite understand. Something about being poor.

—

It's three hours to Agra to see the saddest mausoleum in the world.

This white, lacy, feminine structure is beautiful, cer-tainly. We take our shoes off and walk onto the cool, fleshy marble into the interior and enter one of the greatest monuments to grief. The voices bounce off the low, domed ceiling and a sound echoes back to me from at least one of the chambers of Hell. The sound of grief upon grief for the loss of the only beloved. A death without me. A lonely death and now a life without you.

We walk to the other side of the Taj Mahal and are greeted by a scene of contemporary desolation. A dying river, a murder of crows, the foundations of the never finished, black tomb for the King who lost his power and then his life before it could be built. Slums in the distance.

It is a monument to love. I turn my smallness over in my hands, haunted by this woman. This beloved woman.

—

We are accosted at the train station for money but I am too tired for this.

I plead with the beggars, 'Please go away.'

Grimy, wild children in dresses that once were beautiful but now are so very, very dirty. If they were household rags you'd throw them away. One little girl stands with open hands.

'Which god do you believe in?' she asks suddenly. 'What do you call him?'

'I don't have one. I don't believe in god.'

She doesn't believe me. She laughs at my brilliant joke. 'Everyone believes in god,' she says, smiling. The Duke gives her a samosa and she goes away.

People don't use the bridge to change platforms. They cross over the tracks. Dogs and rats and children all play on the train tracks. One guy is sitting in the middle of the tracks, cross-legged on the ground. Maybe he needs some space. I could do with some space. I find myself wanting to yell, for the love of god, get the dogs and the rats and the children off the tracks. There's a train coming. But it doesn't feel like the train will ever come because it's late and cold and the desolation piles up around me and I'm sure that the man standing over there in the orange scarf will throw himself in front of the train if it ever comes because he looks so lost, so forlorn, so desperate and unloved and unwashed and suddenly more than anything, I need a shower.

—

It's late by the time we get back to the hotel.

The Duke hesitates at the lift. 'Is that the Chancellor and the Lady I can hear at the bar?'

I stop to listen. The Chancellor doesn't frequent bars. Something's happened.

The Chancellor toasts us with her shandy as we approach.

'The Princess got an email today. The Office has spoken. She's been dismissed.'

The Lady raises her wine glass.

'The Princess is dead. Long live the Princess.'

Changi

The name Changi means different things to different people. Changi used to be a prisoner of war camp but conditions have greatly improved since then. Nowadays it is the most comprehensive airport in the world. Changi has general facilities, IT and business services, napping facilities, shower, fitness and spa services, music bar lounges, rest areas, a swimming pool, transit hotel, day tour of Singapore, shops, mechanical foot massages, a movie theatre, a food court, restaurants, video games, children's playground, hair and beauty services, medical services, convenience stores, money changers, a post office, a prayer room, a butterfly garden and of course the nature trail which includes a pond with carp so big you could eat them.

Changi is a city in a dome with its own public transport system. A better public transport system than a lot of major cities. It covers an area of 1300 hectares, with 870 of those hectares claimed from the sea. It has two parallel runways 60 metres wide and 4000 metres long. It has 25 kilometres of taxiway. Handling capacity per annum: 68.7 million passengers. It processes 16,500 bags an hour. Changi never sleeps, never turns out the lights, but no one lives here.

We are part of the festive wonderland as part of a credit card promotion where you can win great prizes including trips to Tokyo and Florida. We are part of one of the colourful displays that make up the kaleidoscope of events. We're sharing the bill with Big Mouse and Friends. We must be the friends.

We put the contents of a small flower shop in our wigs so we can toss pretty relics for the travellers to leave discarded on the ground. We are the colour and movement in the background as people run off to find their gate. We do the show. We eat. We sleep. We do the show. The travellers become ghosts. We walk right through them for they cannot see us. We live in limbo for a while.

On the first day we adjust to the absence of the Princess. Fortunately it's the colour and movement show so we just take out the Princess's colour.

On the second day, as we sit around trestle tables while the Chancellor hands out the new schedules, Edmund finally mentions the Princess.

'Did she go quietly?'

'Who?' asks the Chancellor, but she needn't. We all know to whom Edmund is referring.

'The Princess,' says Edmund. 'Did she make a fuss?'

'Of course she made a fuss. She was put on this earth to make a fuss.'

'What did she do?' asks Edmund.

'She locked herself in her hotel room. I considered calling security but I just slipped her new itinerary under the door and didn't look back.'

'How'd she find out if you didn't see her?'

'The Office called her directly.'

'I'm glad she's gone,' says the Lady.

'So am I,' I say involuntarily and then suddenly feel guilty about the hoops.

'Oh I don't know,' says the Prince. 'She was pretty good in the show.'

'She seemed to think so,' says the Lady.

'It's weird, though,' says Edmund. 'I feel a bit strange now that she's been dismissed. It makes me feel sort of insecure.'

Everyone looks at each other, suddenly feeling precisely the same thing.

'Never fear,' says the Duke, 'you're all safe with me. Except the Generalissimo.'

That doesn't reassure me. Judging from the look on Edmund's face, he doesn't feel so comfortable either.

'Well I won't miss the incessant hula-hooping,' says the Chancellor.

'Or the amount of time it took to check into our rooms,' says the Lady.

'Or the scenes she makes at customs.'

'Especially in America. They have no sense of humour when it comes to air travel in the US. I expected her to get arrested every time.'

'How about the scene on the plane over here?'

'Or the dying swan routine?'

'With a hey-nonny no.'

'Have you heard of Joanne Bach?'

'I think I went to school with her.'

'And the way she'd warm up . . .' And the Lady does an impression. She's a decent mimic.

'And sing to herself! They weren't even real songs.' The Chancellor has a go at one of the Princess's nonsense songs. The Chancellor's impression of the Princess isn't as good as the Lady's.

The tête-à-tête between the Lady and the Chancellor quickly descends into grossly unflattering impersonations of the Princess. They get the laughs but we all know we might feel a touch bad about it later. The group begins to drift away. We leave the Lady and the Chancellor in the dressing room, kicking the memory of the Princess around; performing the final exorcism.

—

On the third day, I see the band from the first check-in line in Melbourne. They look dishevelled and unsteady. I think the guy who caught my phone winks at me but I can't be sure. They step onto the moving walkway, arrange themselves like an album cover and glide into the distance.

When it's time to go, none of us is late for the flight. Not even Edmund.

Seoul

Seoul is roads, so very many roads, lanes, streets, alleys, freeways, highways, expressways, byways, motorways, fairways and drives. The cars, so very, very many cars, inch slowly along the asphalt cross-hatching the city. There are rows of neat apartment blocks in the distance, every distance. A life in Seoul would seem to be spent in small rooms: apartment to car to office to car and back to apartment. The latest military demonstration from the North plays on TV at breakfast. It's unsettling knowing this grand posing is happening just over there, over the demilitarised zone, a most heavily armed border. The crowd on television enthusiastically applaud the perfect marching but no one looks very happy.

Seoul is big, so very, very big. So big, in fact, that the commute from the hotel to the venue takes as long as driving between two small towns in Europe. Fortunately there is a karaoke machine on the bus. The Lady sings 'Amazing Grace', which has more verses than any of us realised. Eventually she finishes at which point Edmund decides to sing 'The Mercy Seat'; which is another very long but not vocally difficult song. He enlists the help of everyone and makes it through with a modicum of decorum but when the Generalissimo decides to sing 'Creep', it's time to find something else to do.

We finally make it to the hotel and scurry to our respective small rooms and change for a night out. We've finished all the shows, sung all the songs on the karaoke bus and will be meeting up with ten French mimes who have been doing shows at the same festival. We're going to meet for drinks in the nightclub part of town. The Prince knows where that is. He assures us that the mimes are not in fact mute, as the Lady has incorrectly assumed, and that out of their unitards these ten French mimes are really quite chatty.

After a taxi ride that is mercifully short, we find a door and descend the stairs into the darkened nightclub below.

Ten French mimes, hedonistic battle-axes of the touring circuit, have made the empty establishment their own. They know the hidden worlds you create when you live slightly out of pace with life. As we do.

So there we are. Ten French mimes and five third-rate acrobats, all unsure about how to begin. The Prince suddenly jumps off a podium at a particularly dramatic point of the music playing in the club and it's on. The two groups pretty much run towards each other and start dancing.

Professional bodies dance in partners, finding pathways along each other's bodies, rivulets of energy: big lifts, aerial stunts and moments of balanced stillness. Although unable to defy gravity, these dancers can at least to be insolent about it.

You know when you're on. When your light is on. And it turns on everyone else. Suddenly the whole world's looking at you and everyone wants to take you home. The universe puts its non-existent hand on your shoulder and says, 'Have who you will, they all want you, have fun.'

Ten French mimes, all standing in a line, I wonder, which one I will make, mine. They each say hello: *'Bon soir,' 'Enchanté,' 'Ça va?'* I dance with one and then another and then another.

The first, Pierre, speaks English and he leads. He turns his head and the intersection of his neck with his chest, the articulation of the atlas with the axis, the line of muscle joining the clavicle, emerges from his neck in an elegant ridge and then a muscle in his jaw contracts. So does something in me. He is old school and knows what it means to make all the moves. Sometimes you just want to be told what to do.

The second, Gascon, speaks no English. He doesn't lead. A conversation is more compelling than a series of commands. He dances easily. He has powerful forearms, the mechanics of his limbs apparent, shifting under his skin as he arrests my spin.

The next three are all called Jean. Jean is quiet and has delicate, expressive hands. Jean is kind and has a contoured back you'd retire to if it were an island while Jean has impeccable manners and white, welcoming teeth placed in a charming overbite.

Renaud shares a name with a car and is creative, unexpected, witty. He has a slender brown body and a casual grace.

Alvin has a light touch and eyes that make him look like he is always on the verge of laughing. He is highly skilled in his clumsiness. His prattfalls are little poems.

Etienne has a hard stomach, furrows of muscles, and a stomach with texture, with definition. He knows where his centre is and how to move it.

Albert has that curve of the inner hip, the external

abdominal oblique muscle, that wholly masculine defini-tion which leads the eye to . . . the eye to . . .

Rene has olive skin, I imagine he is circumcised and of a reassuring size, not too much either way. I imagine the way it will leap into my hand. I imagine the money shot.

'*Qu'est-ce que tu penses de moi pour le moment?*' says Rene.

The Duke appears in front of me.

'You coming? We're off. It's daylight outside.'

And suddenly I am. I'm leaving. As I walk up the stairs back into the morning I wonder what Rene said. I wish I spoke French. Why can't I stop walking away? And then I realise I'm not going home with any of them. I feel my light dimming and then turning off completely. It's all in the timing: dancing, comedy, sex. It's the ones that don't happen that haunt you.

Ghent

The skies of Europe are scored with white contrails. You can tell where you are by simply looking up. We stay in Ghent in between times. We tend to start here, finish here and stay here when there is nowhere else to be. We know how to get around here. We know where the shops are. We even know where Kortrijksepoortstraat leads to, even if we can't spell it.

Ghent is a town with a great silhouette. I love the way the edges of the seemingly two-dimensional façades of the buildings meet the storybook blue sky. It's a town you see illustrated for children. Ghent feels as familiar as if I grew up here. My favourite meal. My favourite fourteenth-century view. Returning to a room with a view of other windows with views of other windows. Foreign keyboards that make you write in an accent. Dusk at eleven at night. The plastic key to my hotel room says *Bonne Nuit*, Good Night, *Gute Nacht* and *Buona Notte* and I feel so pleased to be in a country that can wish me good night in so many languages.

Ghent is in Belgium. Belgium is a country but more often used as a unit of measurement: 'The Kalahari Desert is as big as Belgium' or 'the Amazon has been cleared, an area the size of Belgium' or even 'If the earth was hit by a one kilometre asteroid, it would leave a hole the size of Belgium'. A Belgium is big but not as big as, say, a Russia.

We meet for dinner. The great thing about being on the road is you always have to eat out.

The Duchess has replaced the Princess. She's an outgoing blonde with a bracing personality who loves to dress up. She has a unique taste in outfits. She has been known to attract comments in the street. Comments such as *'Tirate a un poso'*, which means 'go throw yourself in a hole', *'Tu eres más feo que el culo de un mono'*, which becomes 'you are uglier than the backside of a monkey', and of course *'Vous avez le cerveau d'un sandwich au fromage'*, which loosely translated means 'you have the brain of a cheese sandwich'. European women can be so cruel.

We order mussels that come in buckets and famous Belgian beers that make everyone's eyes glitter, heralding the onset of profound drunkenness. We are sitting by the canal that makes its way through the town.

'I do love a good canal,' says the Duke.

'Can you not talk like that at the dinner table?' says the Chancellor.

'It was an innocent comment. It's your beady little brain that went to the backdoor.'

The Chancellor makes a face.

'I went shopping today,' says the Duchess brightly. 'I bought frivolous writing gear and campy bibelots.'

'What's a bibelot?' asks the Prince.

'No idea but according to the man at the shop, I bought one.'

'It's a small decorative ornament or trinket,' says the Duke.

'Show-off,' says the Chancellor.

'Did you know that Belgium only has seven kilometres of coastline?' says the Duchess.

The Duke narrows his eyes. 'Who told you that?'

'The man at the shops today. He was very talkative.'

'I think he was joking.'

'I bet you it's true.'

'It's sixty-seven.'

'Twenty-seven,' corrects Edmund.

'One hundred and seven,' I say. I have no idea how long the coastline is but I feel like joining in.

The Prince leaves the table to go to the gents. He's a fine specimen of a young man and all the women and some of the men watch his small continent of a back recede into the restaurant. The Duchess seems particularly interested.

'You had better take care. He is very fascinating,' purrs the Duke in the vicinity of her ear.

'He's a bit young for me,' says the Duchess. 'He'd be fun for a moment but I can't see myself bringing him home for Christmas.'

'Romantic sex isn't the only pleasure, darling,' says the Duke.

We all pause and consider this for a moment.

—

Tomorrow is a day off so we celebrate by going to every bar we come across. We come across a lot of bars. Finally we find ourselves in a place called Suite Sixteen. The drinks are expensive but in return we get a splendid view of the high-tech open fireplace.

The Duke, Duchess, Prince and Lady are cackling by

the fireplace. I join Edmund at the bar for a change of pace. Edmund is notoriously successful with the ladies. He presents as being single on tour protected by the age-old 'what happens on tour, stays on tour'. The thing is, you wouldn't think he was such a Lothario by looking at him. He's pleasing on the eye but no Adonis with flashing muscles and sculptured smiles. He has big feet. And his ears stick out a bit. So do his teeth.

'Anyone caught your eye this evening?' I enquire.

'Maybe,' replies Edmund, looking at me from under lidded eyes.

'What's your secret?'

'Which secret might this be then?'

'The secret of your success with women. I've never fallen under your spell so I don't know.'

'You will.'

'You wish.'

'You wish.'

'You wish.'

We invoke wishes on each other for a while.

'You will.'

'Edmund, we'll see.'

'You will.'

'Can we go back to talking about your technique to help me in my search for meaningless sex?'

'I thought you were looking for love.'

'I've given that up and now look only for misspending my youth with an array of handsome young men.'

Edmund decides to dispense his own special wisdom.

'It's about reading people. See that woman over there?'

Edmund indicates a small blonde in the corner laughing with her girlfriends.

'Yeah.'

'She's not interested tonight. I bet she has a boyfriend at home and things are going fine. No point. It would be a waste of time trying anything with her.'

'How can you tell that?'

'It's in the smile.'

'How about that woman over there?'

I point out a stunning redhead by the fire.

'Absolutely not. I suspect a troubled break-up. You can see it in the way she holds her shoulders. She's still too angry for the likes of me and she's not drinking. Too hard. Defences are in place.'

'Are we talking about war or seduction here?'

'Same principles.'

I catch a stunning brunette flash Edmund a promising toss of the hair.

'I think that's my cue,' says Edmund.

'If you do get lucky tonight, and you probably will, could you do it at her place?'

Edmund and I have to share a room in Ghent this time. Gentse Feesten is on and rooms are at a premium.

As he slides down the bar he says, over his shoulder, 'You know me, discretion is my middle name.'

Alone, I consider my drink and consider having another one. I look up and two young men are gesturing to the bar stools either side of me.

'Do you mind?' says the taller one of the two.

'No. Of course not.'

'Would you like a drink?'

'Okay.'

'This is Arnaud and my name is Florent.'

I tell them my name and catch Edmund giving me the eyebrow. He seems to be doing very well with the brunette. I go to put my elbow on the bar. It misses.

The elbow misses two more times until I find purchase on the burnished steel.

'So, where are you from?' asks Florent, a pleasant blond with all of the requisite muscles in all the right places.

'Australia.'

'So you're from Australia. We've been to Australia.'

'Really? Do you know, in Australia, we have cattle stations the size of Belgium?'

Framed by Florent and Arnaud's handsome faces, I notice Edmund and the brunette kissing passionately by the high-tech fireplace.

I sit down in slow motion and narrowly avoid missing the seat when Arnaud puts his hand on my knee and Florent steals a kiss. I really didn't see this coming. And now it's here. So quickly.

'This is what we do in Europe,' he says into my neck.

'Kiss strange girls in bars,' I say, distracted by the sensations on my collarbone. 'I think that might be an international phenomenon.'

But I don't resist. And then Arnaud kisses me and suddenly I'm presented with a very interesting erotic proposal. I don't want to hurt anyone's feelings and I've never been good at making decisions. I make the decision by not making one.

'Should we go someplace else?' asks Florent.

'Okay,' I respond, pliable and very, very drunk.

We leave the bar and someone decides we are going to my hotel but I can't remember where it is. I'm having trouble telling my Hoogstraat from my Holstraat.

We pause on a bridge in a passionate embrace plus one. I'm enjoying being the centre of attention. This is so unlike me. We cavort down Graffiti Street. I'm enjoying being lost.

We finally find the hotel and go upstairs. I go to the bathroom. I catch my breath; decide I've come this far so I might as well see it through to its conclusion. I come out of the bathroom and the two lads are both sitting on the couches naked and giggling.

I hear Edmund's key in the lock. I race to the door and put my full weight against it, madly hoping he'll think the door is stuck or something, anything, so he will just go away and maybe stay somewhere else tonight. After a short, silent struggle, he opens it anyway.

Edmund stands in the doorway looking at the two nude men on the couch.

'Hello there,' says Florent. Arnaud waves cheerily.

Edmund screams like a very little girl and runs off down the corridor.

I look at Florent and Arnaud and we hang there in silence and stillness and then, as if cued, the two boys are upon me.

We start moving in earnest. I commit to the act. I'm being fucked and fucking in the same moment. This is about cocks and cunts and do it to me big boy. It is raw, recreational, anonymous sex. We make semaphore with our bodies. We spell out words with the positions we get into. It's a strangely liberating experience. There are more hands and mouths than usual. A fabulous sensory over-load. Part of me is shocked at what I'm doing but another part of me finds it incredibly funny like a joke that goes on and on with bigger and better punchlines. The rest of me isn't thinking anything much but, rather, being swept up in it all. They are gentle with me. They carefully avoid each other. It really is all about me.

'What's that?' says Florent. 'I think I can hear someone at the door again.'

We freeze mid-thrust like rabbits in headlights. Naked rabbits doing something we hope our mothers will never hear about.

'It's nothing,' says one of the boys. I've stopped bothering to attribute hands and mouths and voices to anyone any more. After a moment, we continue.

———

In the morning we sit around in our nudity for a while, dressed in our best manners.

'Would you like a shower?' I ask the boys.

'After you,' says Florent, with a little bow.

'No, no, after you.'

'Thank you.'

'You should come and see the show I perform in.'

'We don't need to. Can't beat the performance you put in last night.'

I laugh. We will never meet each other again. It was strange and funny and has no consequences in the bright light of morning.

———

Edmund and I meet each other for breakfast at a café with limited seating. The kind of small café where you sit at other people's tables and read from their newspaper. Thankfully, we have a table to ourselves.

'About last night . . .' I say.

'You should have put a sock on the door or something.'

'I'm sorry about that. I'm sorry you had to see that.'

'Not as sorry as I am.'

'Where'd you stay?'

'The Prince put me up.'

'You didn't mention . . .'

'No.'

'I thought you were going off with the brunette.'

'Didn't work out.'

'That's not like you. What happened?'

'Nothing happened.'

'I know that. Why did nothing happen?'

Edmund sighs. 'Don't tell anyone, okay. It was going really well and we started kissing. But then I noticed there was something in the kiss that was different. More full on. Then my hands did the walking and walked into . . .' He shudders.

'What?'

'Something I never, ever want to touch again unless it's my own.'

'What?'

'She had a penis. She was a he. I kissed a man.'

'Passionately kissed a man. That was no peck on the cheek from where I was standing.'

'Standing in between those two men.'

'Yeah, okay.'

'Look, let's keep last night to ourselves.'

'Okay, I won't tell if you don't tell.'

'Agreed.'

We studiously turn our attention to breakfast.

Oostende

Once known in the nineteenth century as the 'Queen of the Belgium Seaside Resorts', Oostende is a little tatty around the edges these days. A sign in front of a local travel agent says 'Our staff will gladly help you out of the country'. Apparently Belgium is a country you travel through, on the way to somewhere else.

Oostende has a fine sand beach, wind that is never in short supply and the biggest seagulls I have ever seen in my life. I try not to catch their eye in case they think I'm looking for a fight and decide to rough me up a bit.

Our warm-up space is a gorgeous building with high ceilings and an old, wooden floor. That's what Europe has, an abundance of rooms – beautiful, beautiful rooms. I guess that's where all the forests went.

We begin to warm up. Bodies unfold all over the room. Limbs stretch in all directions. Become apparent.

The Duke spirals his way into standing. You wouldn't think to look at him walking along the street, but the Duke is a very graceful and flexible man, almost delicate. The delicate assassin. He disappears out the door for a cigarette.

Edmund immerses himself in the company class being led by the Lady. He loves the long lines and subtle shifts and changes of direction. He's a ballerina from way back. Sometimes he finds a way to hang in the air longer than he should. This is a young man who can dance without a prop like a motorbike or a surfboard or a ball.

The Lady sets a lovely phrase of movement interlaced with some sweeping high kicks. I lean into the corners of the circle. I send my legs through the range of my personal hemisphere. I enjoy banging myself in the chest with my legs. The Prince sidles up to me and loudly whispers, 'There were three in the bed and the little one said . . .'

I look at the Prince in shock and accidentally kick myself in the head.

'Was that you at the door?'

'Sure was.'

'You saw . . .'

'Everything.'

'Have you told anyone else?'

The Prince flashes me a wicked grin.

'Have you?'

He kicks into a handstand and runs away from me, upside down. By the time I catch up to him, he's rolled back onto his feet again.

'Have you? Have you told the girls?'

He sidesaults away from me.

'Because if you've told the girls, this is going to be a very long tour for me.'

The Prince clambers up the window onto one of the exposed beams in the ceiling and beams down at me. Damned monkey man.

'You wait there. I'm just going to go and kill Edmund and then I'll be back for you.'

The Prince jumps down beside me like a big cat.

'No one else knows. Hey, I admire you. You go girl.'

'I'm not usually that kind of a girl.'

'Sure you're not.'

'I'm not.'

'Was it fun?'

'Keep what you saw to yourself?'

'You can trust me.'

I'm not so sure that I can but there's nothing I can do about it now. Except plot revenge on Edmund. Edmund the bastard. There. I've said it. I weigh up different revenge scenarios as I go back to my stretching.

My body is wound tight today. In the mornings it takes a good hour before I can stand up straight. You always work with at least one injury in this business. There's always something wrong. Something tight, some ache, something you have to keep your eye on. Something to work through. The pain moves around your body, visiting different territories: the back area, the shoulder region, the ankle district. I've had some injuries longer than some of my friendships.

I wander over to the mirrors to put on the heavy make-up. I sit next to the Lady. She is in a talkative mood tonight.

She tells me about her childhood. I don't know why. I didn't ask.

'My mum had me when she was sixteen,' she says as she applies the base coat to her face.

'Sixteen?'

'Yeah. Dad left before I was born and I've never met him.'

'Never met him?'

'He went to take the dog for a walk and never came back. Mum never saw the dog again either.'

'Right.'

'Mum and I drove past the service station where he works one day but I only saw him for a moment when I was hanging out the window of the car. He has dark hair.'

'Like you.'

'Then he moved to the Northern Territory.'

'Right.'

'Then Mum changed her name to Sun Beam.'

'Sunbeam? Like the toaster?'

'And then we travelled around the country in a Kombi.'

Apparently the Lady didn't go to school for a couple of years during this period. She speaks of riding horses along the beach and living in a commune and darker things. The details and the dates don't match up but some of it must be the truth. Either way her childhood was a was not a happy one. I don't know why she is confiding in me like this. We've never been particularly close.

The Lady glues a fake eyelash in place.

'I had a sister. Younger sister. Mum liked her better than me. Her dad sent money. My dad never sent us any money. As a child I wasn't much of an earner. We went to a picnic. With mum's family. It was in bushland just out of Byron Bay. The park had a great big pond. My sister and I were playing with a ball with our cousins. Just throwing it to each other. I threw the ball to my sister but it went past her and fell into the pond. My sister ran after the ball. She ran into the pond. She got caught in some rushes by the edge. It was too deep for her. She splashed around like a dog that doesn't know how to swim. I screamed and screamed. I thought someone would hear me. No one came. After a while the splashing stopped.'

'She?'

'When mum came to find us, it was too late.'

The Lady puts her wig on and shuffles it into place. She puts a pin in her hair.

'I'm so sorry to hear that,' I say, not knowing what else to say.

A silence hangs in the air between us. It's not a comfortable silence. The Lady eventually speaks.

'No, I'm joking. My sister lives in Adelaide now.'

She smiles at me in the mirror. I try to return the smile. My mouth can manage it but my eyes have trouble joining in.

—

The spotlight suddenly illuminates the Lady. She's a powerful, gothic actor, I'll give her that much. She knows how to manifest dark places in the human soul for our viewing pleasure. She extends a bony arm and her hand shapes the air as a potter does clay. In the distance, I see a flash on the horizon. Her other arm shoots out and it is like she can move the material world by simply gesticulating wildly. Dark clouds gather swiftly around us. She pulls her arms back to her centre and a clap of thunder startles us all. We can see the whites of her eyes. And then it starts to rain. Heavy, insistent, dangerous for us, rain. The Generalissimo gives the sign to come down with a wave of his hand and we all carefully descend. The crowd scurries for shelter. We start to pack up. The Lady appears beside me.

'I am magic, you know,' she says, and pins me with an unblinking, wide-eyed stare.

'Looks like you are.'

'But I won't hurt you.'

'Glad to hear it.'

'I like you. I think we should be friends.'

'Yes. I'd like that.'

I look for something to do by the truck. Edmund is heaving lead into the back of the van.

'Need a hand there, Edmund?'

I hurry off.

León

Gaudi designed the bank and the Cathedral has gigantic storks building nests on the towers and turrets. Melancholic beauty. Gothic splendour. León's a lovely little town.

A man sings under the great, black sky. He sings upset songs. He seems to be in despair at the end of every number. Nothing ever seems to work out for him. Always terribly disappointed about something. He loses his coat, his shirt and finally his chair in a series of bigger and unhappier finishes. The crowd loves him. His cries fill the dark night. All night.

The Duchess makes a proclamation.

'I want to go dancing.'

The Prince is dancing a little already.

'I'm in.'

'Me too,' says Edmund.

The Lady calls from the mirror.

'I'll just put on my make up.'

The Duchess looks to the Duke.

'For a short while,' says the Duke.

—

We throw ourselves in among the crowd and start dancing to the cheap tricks of electronic music. The people, so many people. I catch brief glimpses of living statues in vivid colour. A man with black hair falling into his blue eyes, an ancient stone torso made flesh and a pale beauty newly emerged from the sea.

On the other side of a small forest of limbs, the Duchess is dancing with the Prince. She overestimates a shimmy and falls over on the dance floor, with her legs in the air. Fortunately, tonight she's decided on the underwear.

After the obligatory handstand on the dance floor, the Prince disappears into the writhing mass of bodies. The Duchess is up again momentarily and starts dancing with a swarthy man in the corner. Edmund grooves past. The Duchess dacks Edmund as he passes without missing a beat. Edmund pulls his trousers up from his ankles in horror and skulks away.

The Lady appears by my side.

'Where's the Duke?'

'Never came back from the gents,' I say.

'How long ago was that?'

'About an hour.'

'Do you think he's coming back?'

'I don't think so.'

'I feel faint.'

'Have you eaten today?'

'I'm going home.'

And with this, the Lady falls over. She slides into unconsciousness gracefully right down her centre line. Edmund magically catches her fall from nowhere. He has his coat on.

'I'm off. Should I take her?' He indicates the swooning woman in his arms.

'I think so.'

He disappears into the crowd with the Lady mostly in his arms. The Duchess drapes herself on me like an ill-fitting coat.

'Whereisothers?'

'Gone.'

'Gone?'

'Home.'

'Home?'

'Had enough?'

'Had enough.'

She puts her face very close to mine.

'You know, I would never sleep with a man who wore plastic travellers sandals with a Velcro buckle.'

I wear her to the nearest exit.

—

The Duchess is climbing the cathedral. She's pretty far up.

'Come down,' I yell.

'No. All is lies.'

She calls out to the storks nesting in the turrets.

'When I was a little girl I used to scream and shout. When I was a little girl I used to scream and shout. When I was . . .'

'I'll come up and get you.'

'I was good. I was so good I was great. I found out how to fly. I had no fear. I came as near to flying as anyone can manage without an airplane. Turning in space. Bending time. Following the line. I was National Champion. Nothing has ever felt as good as being National Champion. But then Mum got sick. And then

I woke up one morning and didn't believe any more. And then I wasn't National Champion. Now I'm not National Champion, I don't know who I am.'

'I know who you are,' I shout. 'You're the one hanging off the cathedral.'

And then she calmly reaches down and, with infinite slowness, does a handstand on a ledge of the Church. She balances in the air and then moves onto one arm, testing the balance with her fingertips and then folding the rest of her limbs against her body. A stork launches into the sky somewhere above her. She stands as resolute as a saint and then slowly, deliberately finds her feet. She stands for a moment and then does a layout off the side of the building. She lands it. On cobblestones. In high heels.

'Nice stunt.'

'Thank you,' the Duchess says with a triumphant smile. And then trips over an empty can.

'I'malright . . . alright. . . right.'

We walk on in silence. Well I walk. The Duchess staggers.

—

At the entrance to the hotel we can still hear the sad man singing in the distance. A flapping sound near the doorway distracts the Duchess. The sound emanates from a pigeon with a broken wing. The Duchess raises her bag. I am aghast.

'What are you doing?'

'I'm going to kill it.'

'Don't kill it. We might be able to save it.'

'No point.'

'What do you mean, no point?'

'It won't ever be able to fly again. No point in living if you can't fly.'

'Just hang on. I'll get someone from the hotel.'

The bag remains in the air.

'Please, please don't. Please.'

The bag slowly descends.

I catch the eye of the man behind the desk and steer the Duchess towards the lifts. I lean her in the corner of the elevator. She begins to fold into herself. As the door closes, she slides onto the floor.

The sad man comes to the end of another song. Small finish. The crowd starts chanting.

Madrid

We have a day off in Madrid after a season performing in the middle of Plaza Mayor, which
is, apparently, the centrepiece of life in Madrid where
people sit outside at tables under umbrellas and sip cold
drinks. The plaza is elegance personified with its slate
spires and wrought iron façades but apparently it wasn't
always like this. During the Inquisition there were burn-
ings at the stake in the north corner and hangings in
the south. And then a fire consumed the square so they
decided to turn it into a plaza for bullfights. The Spanish
taste for entertainment must have changed over the
years. The crowd seemed to enjoy the show despite the
lack of a body count at the end.

It is a warm day. A warm, sunny day verging on the
uncomfortable and I'm with the Duchess sitting in
the stalls of an arena. The crowd is awash with elderly
Spanish couples waving to each other with their white
hankies and tourists feeling all cheerful with homely
associations of football matches back home. We have
cushions to sit on, corn to eat and beers in hand. A lovely
day for a bullfight.

The band plays a bright and brassy tune. The first bull
runs into the arena. The crowd lets out an almighty

cheer. It has colourful ribbons at its neck. Sorry, that's in its neck. There is a knife sunk deep into his flesh and this is what the ribbons are attached to. They cascade prettily behind him as he runs around the ring.

Men with big pink capes stab him and then run away to hide behind wooden barriers. Then a man on a blind-folded horse enters the arena. The horse wears a kind of armour and has been trained to resist the impact of the enraged beast trying to gorge its side. Apparently the horse has to be blindfolded or it would be too afraid of the bull. The man on the horse stabs the bull for a while with a long pike. And then the blind horse ambles out of the torture yards.

Finally the matador comes out. Arrogant, swinging, he looks straight ahead as he marches. The crowd goes wild. Well, not the tourists. We are pale and shaky and slumped in our seats. The matador dances with death. Not his own death but someone else's. He has a small red cape and very big sword.

My tears begin at the first clumsy death. The bull stumbles, deeply afraid, into the barrier. He bleeds from his mouth. The crowd cheers along each pass, each stab. He spits blood and, I imagine, only then realises what he suspects: he's dying. His end is moments away and in this moment of clarity he sags and dies.

The second bull has an awkward, almost comical death. The crowd laughs. I know these animals by the colour of their coats and the circumstances of their passing.

The third one doesn't even make it past the first fes-tive ribbons fastened jauntily to the knife in his neck. He keeps falling over. He can't get up. The knife has been put in at the wrong angle and has disabled the bull too much too soon, by mistake. He keeps falling over and simply can't get up. The guys in the pink capes look confused for a moment. Maybe the bull knows the routine and decides to skip the next bit. Ends the same anyway. They stab him to death where he lies, the horses drag him off and it doesn't count as a bullfight. A death that doesn't count. Do they cry out when they die? I am too far away to hear if they do. And I'm glad, at least, for that. Another bull takes his place. The band strikes up.

I mutter something about going to the bathroom. The Duchess can't tear her eyes away from the arena. She's a Taurus so I think watching her totem die over and over again is really getting her down. Birds are one thing, her star sign is quite another. I think she might be in at least mild shock. There is no colour in her face. I find my way out of the stadium.

Disorientated and distressed, I stumble around and around the corridors looking for a way out. A tall man with a big cigar stands by a wall. I sag against it.

'So, how are you enjoying the bullfight?' asks the man with the cigar. With each word, small puffs of smoke punctuate his words. He speaks English and guesses that I do too. Maybe it's the way I hold my mouth or something.

'I've never seen anything like it.'

He grins and takes a puff of his cigar.

'Tell me. I have to know, why do the Spanish love the bullfight?' I ask in a small voice.

He stubs out his cigar as he answers.

'The bull is the only animal that gets to fight before they die. Chickens don't get to fight, pigs don't get to fight but the bull, the bull dies honourably.'

'What happens to the bull after you kill it?'

'We eat it.'

'That's good,' I say weakly but I still don't feel any better about it all.

Alicante

The Duke is flustered.

'Right, then, the presenter still wants us to do the show.'

The temperature is 36 degrees so it's just under the hot weather call. One more notch on the gauge and we could cancel but no, the mercury refuses the single degree that would send us back to our air-conditioned hotel rooms.

We are impaled in the sky. The audience, far away in the slightly less hot shade of the trees, must be wondering why we're doing anything at all in this weather. We are wondering exactly the same thing.

I climb down after the show and catch my reflection in a shop window. I am monster face. A swamp creature. The whole greasy mask has slipped from my features and is now a second face on my chest.

'*¿Qué piensa usted de mi ahora?*' trills the Duke.

'I know, I know. What do you think of me so far?'

Valencia

The cleaning lady hoovers a threat on the other side of the door. She knocks and her head appears. I wearily wave a not now from under the covers and she goes away. It's amazing how much sleeping in I do in beautiful places. May you live all the days of your life indeed.

I'm tired. All last night I could hear the crazy sounds of bands wandering though the streets. I don't think Spaniards ever sleep. Fireworks so loud I thought the civil war had broken out again.

Spain. The land of the eternal morning face. There is first morning at the traditional time and then after siesta there is another morning. Two mornings in one day. I'm never good in the morning. How the Spanish get anything done, I do not know.

I finally get up for the second morning and walk around the room in my plain face. The face I use around the house when no one else is looking. It is the kind of achingly beautiful day that makes me feel lonely.

There is this silence that descends, or surrounds you, when you walk around someone else's country if you can't speak their language. You can't ask for directions, chat to a stranger or understand snatches of conversation when you walk by. I stalk the streets in a sphere of quietude.

I eventually make it to the beach. There is no spectacular sunset. The sun just goes down. It's still warm without the sun. I play in the shallows of the dark ocean. It is bath water warm and the surface is still. I don't go in too deep. Never trust the ocean; even this swimming pool sea.

At a restaurant a man approaches me. He gestures that he needs a light. I accommodate him. He takes a seat and joins me at the table. We smoke in silence for a while. He turns his head and I notice his long, elegant neck. I put out my cigarette. He looks at me intently. And then he kisses me. He just kisses me. Or we kiss. Either way I am complicit. He takes me by the hand. He leads me down the street. I follow. We come to a hotel; a much nicer hotel than mine. He leads me through the foyer and then to his room. A suit is hanging on the door of the wardrobe. I capitulate. I surrender. I yield. We never say a word as he leads me to the tightly made bed. We roll around like teenagers and don't go all the way.

In the daylight I tumble from the bed. Our act is left cartwheeling around itself.

It spins and fades.

'Thank you,' he says, 'it was a pleasure meeting you.'

He speaks English. I laugh at the exquisite joke. There is nothing more to say.

—

As I make my way through the baking streets of Valencia I think about time. Time runs, it doesn't amble. I spend so much time concerned with time — being on time, mainly — and yet I wonder where it all goes and if there isn't something better that I should be doing with it. And that what I have just done may have been a waste of my time. I think about getting to Newgrange to distract myself.

Horn

God made the world but the Dutch made Holland. A land of flat horizons bereft of hills, decorated with belts of vibrant colour, scored with tiny canals and the odd stone fence. The lowlands reclaimed from the sea. The buildings lean into the street to keep the rain off the people at the front door. They have such polite houses here.

Horn is pleasant. A personable small town. We swim in a part of the ocean that has been captured by the land. Seventy years have passed and now it's become a freshwater lake. From sea to land to very big pond. *The Dukes of Hazzard* plays non-stop on the TV, which perhaps gives an insight into the Dutch sense of humour.

We've all met for dinner and everyone is bone-tired. We travelled here yesterday and have just finished two shows. The mood is quiet and possibly dangerous. The Prince does a desultory handstand on the street before going into the restaurant. His heart is not in it. The Duke takes a breath through his cigarette.

'So there we were trying to find La Guerre, you know, the train station in Paris and we're struggling to get through the traffic, the usual nightmare, and we get lost. So I ask Edmund to ask a man on the side of the road where the station is and Edmund shouts at this man,

"*Ou est la guerre? Ou est la guerre?*" The man looks confused and walks off and Edmund says, "Why didn't he answer me?" It's because Edmund was asking the man "Where's the war? Where's the war?"'

'I'm going to learn Spanish instead,' says Edmund.

'Maybe you should start with English first,' says the Duchess.

'It always confounds me how you can be on, in this flat land full of tall and gooty men,' says the Duke after I attract another pleasant smile from a stranger passing by.

'Gooty isn't a word.'

'Yes it is. It means gangly and goofy.'

It's true. Tall, lean men on the street speak to me in Dutch. When I answer them in English, they instantly change languages. Just like that. They turn a switch in their head. I can almost hear the click. Helpful strangers riding bicycles engage me in conversation in the language of my choosing.

'Well, which country turns your light on?' I ask.

'All of them, darling.'

The bill arrives. The Chancellor takes it quickly. She reads it and passes it on. Everyone takes turns to put money on the plate.

The Duchess re-counts the money.

'We're short. It's a ten per cent tip in this country, folks. Did anyone not include the tip?'

'The service was slow,' says the Prince.

'It's designed to make you feel at home. That's why it's slow.'

The Prince throws more money on the plate. I surreptitiously do the same.

'We're still short. Chancellor, what did you have?'

'I put in for half my sandwich because Edmund ate the other half.'

'You didn't want it. You offered it to me. I didn't know I was meant to pay for it,' says Edmund, deeply affronted.

'Well I think you should pay for half of it. It's not on my plate anymore, is it?'

'If I'd known you expected me to pay for it, I wouldn't have eaten it.'

The Duke weighs in on the issue.

'You can't do that, Chancellor.'

'Yes I can.'

'No you can't. It's completely fucked,' says the Duchess, getting ready for a brawl.

The Chancellor looks around the table at a group of very unfriendly faces getting ready to tear her meaty throat out.

'Okay, but I don't think it's fair.' She resentfully reaches into her purse.

Now the bill has been settled we all go in separate directions. Edmund, the Duke and I decide to find a bar for a digestive. We find one that looks cosy not far from the restaurant with large, friendly wooden tables.

'Marvellous, bloody marvellous,' says the Duke. 'This is a living rather than a job.'

Edmund and I nod our heads in ready agreement as the first mouthful of alcohol tricks us into feeling everything is well in the world.

The Duke notices Edmund's shoes.

'Nice shoes, Edmund. Where did you get them?'

'Madrid.'

'I grew up without shoes,' says the Duke, 'not that you need them in New Zealand. No snakes or spiders or bindis in our meadows.'

'I had to wash my school uniform every night,' says Edmund. 'I didn't have a change of clothes until I got to high school. Single mum, three kids, money was tight. I did a paper round when I was in primary school. Every bit helped.'

'Where was your dad?' I ask.

'Out west somewhere. I dunno. Are your parents together?'

'Despite themselves,' I say.

'Brothers? Sisters?'

'Two brothers.'

'I have eight brothers and sisters,' says the Duke, 'and Mum took in a couple of our cousins because their father was knocking them about so that made eleven of us.'

'Eleven kids. How very eighteenth century,' I say and immediately wish I hadn't. I try to cover it with a question.

'What did your dad do?'

'Odd jobs. And Mum worked at the local supermarket. She loved it. They've just bought their first house.'

'Wow. How old are they?'

'In their seventies. I guess they didn't want to tie themselves down to a mortgage too early in life.'

'Did you get along with your dad?'

'He was rough.'

'How rough?'

'Rough.'

'My mum was rough,' Edmund says. 'I got in big trouble one day for sleeping in and missing my paper round. She threw me and I caught the side of the table.' He raises his shirt and his ribs are uneven. The Duke and I look at his torso in silence. Edmund pulls down his shirt.

'Another round?' says Edmund, suddenly keen to change the subject.

The Duke spins his empty wine glass between his fingers.

'Why not?'

'What was it like coming out to your parents?' I ask the Duke.

'Well, when I told Dad. I said, "Dad, I'm gay" and he said nothing so I went, "so, then . . . well, that's all really I . . . do you want to . . . no . . . I guess not . . . I'll be going then . . . Okay . . ." He just kept looking at the TV and never answered me. When I told Mum she said, "I thought so. I hope it makes you happy".'

'And has it?'

'It has.' He raises his drink and three glasses meet in the centre of the table.

An accordion begins playing outside in the street, slow and mannered. We go outside to see. An old man on a low stool is playing an unhinged melody. It is a preposterous tune. The music sings non compos mentis but the old man looks sane enough.

Lit by the big moon and framed by the pretty, pretty street, Edmund begins dancing. Slowly at first he sweeps his arms across the horizon and arches his back like a matador and then stumbles into a leap, which spirals into a balance. He stands on one leg and his limbs stretch out to the points of the compass, all the points of the compass, turning slowly. He submits to gravity once more and his dance picks up momentum.

The Duke joins in. He begins a circular, introspective pattern. He becomes immersed in spirals, every spiral. He spins into and out of himself. They both give form to things that words can't describe. I join in the dance. Three demented figures cavorting around an empty street and an old man squeezing the life into his accordion.

Amsterdam

The streets teem with tourists. I haven't met anyone who actually lives here. The locals must live further out of town and generally not work in hospitality. Maybe they go abroad for the summer. I certainly would in their position.

Rangy groups of English lads drink beer. They drink their beer on specially modified bicycles that allow group drunkenness and exercise at the very same time. They sit around an internal table with pedals and it still hangs together more or less as a bike. The guide sits higher up and makes sure they don't pedal into a canal. I wonder why you'd bother drinking beer in Amsterdam. There are so many other illicit pleasures on offer here. I would think drinking would be the last thing you would do. I guess some people just really love being drunk.

I'm sitting in a window at a café where the coffee is truly awful and the dope far too strong. I just wanted a giggle, not full body paralysis. People are looking at me as they walk by. I guess in Amsterdam you're allowed to look in windows.

The girls in the windows surround the Catholic Church. St Nick the patron saint of sailors is apparently also the saint of turning a blind eye. I walk past the

Prostitution Information Centre and turn down one of the narrow streets that lead to the red light district and suddenly get incredibly intimidated. Some of the girls notice my . . . my . . . I don't know what it is . . . fear . . . titillation . . . wonder? They laugh and call out to me. I won't be beaten. They are just women in underwear. I make my way down the street and try not to catch their eyes. They smile and wave cheerfully at me anyway.

In one window there is a woman who is all flashing thighs and long nails and blonde hair. She looks from her window with a mixture of aggression and vulnerability. The tiny room behind her has a bed and a bathroom. And that's all. A man, nondescript of course, knocks on her door and she pulls her curtains together.

In another window two middle-aged women read the paper. They sit like an old married couple. Trade must be slower for them now they're over twenty-one but they still seem to manage to pay the rent. Where do working girls go when they retire, I wonder? A nice place in the countryside with smaller windows and bigger rooms maybe?

—

The Prince wants to go to an S&M club. Those of us up for adventure, any adventure, agree to go. We search through our luggage for things black and leathery. I have faux leather pants. Faux in this instance means plastic. I bought the pants on a whim in Ghent. Never thought I'd have an occasion to wear them but here it is. We all decide to go except the Chancellor, who turns pale at the suggestion, and the Generalissimo but we never invite him anywhere.

The Lady insists upon doing my make-up. I'm not keen. I know how to do my make-up. I've been doing my own make-up for years. But there is no getting out of it.

'Close your eyes,' she commands. I comply. She wipes my face with foundation in short, rough strokes.

'You know, you should wear more girly shirts.'

'Girly shirts?'

'You know, ruffles, frills, lace, low necklines.'

'I think a low neckline would be wasted on me.'

'You are quite flat-chested,' she agrees. 'You could wear a scarf,' she adds helpfully. 'Men like scarves.'

'Do they really?'

'They do. Look down.'

The Lady firmly applies what feels like a lot of eye shadow.

'There. All done.'

I open my eyes. She has done my make-up exactly the way she does her own.

'That looks better,' she coos. I look like a drag queen. I decide to be a very well mannered drag queen.

'Thank you, Lady. I look . . . I look . . . thank you, Lady.'

—

We are standing in line outside a club called Paddles. The Duke is dressed in a mesh shirt. Mesh never seems to go out of fashion in Europe. Fortunately the Duke has a body that can wear a mesh creation straight out of the bowels of the 1980s and still look good. Damned clothes horse.

'*Wat denkt u zover van mij?*' he says.

The fact that the Duke knows any Dutch is truly

impressive. Dutch is such a hard language to pronounce with all of those coughing sounds. You pronounce Van Gogh quite differently from the way I was taught in school. The man in the line behind us helpfully translates.

'Your friend said, "What do you think of me so far?"'

Also standing in the queue is a stunning young woman with the strongest jawline and the longest legs in the highest shoes. Just beneath her miniskirt I can see small, controlled cuts on her thighs. She notices me noticing and pulls on her skirt. Her shoes are very impractical. You certainly couldn't go bushwalking in those nine-inch heels. A trip to the corner store would be challenge enough. Whatever world we are stepping into, these people seem to take it very seriously.

The music is loud and it is dark in here. Very, very dark. But it's relaxed. Super relaxed. Cheerful and friendly even. I surmise that once you have a dodgy predilection brought into the light (or half-light in this venue), it creates a sense of community and personal relief. The fact that you can be your strange little self in public creates a room of strangers happy to say hello. Friendly strangers in homemade chain mail and gimp masks.

There is a show of sorts. A well-built man submits to a dominatrix oozing fatly from her leather corset. Stillness and showmanship. He is sitting very still and she is using her whip like a . . . well, a whip. She doesn't seem to have to do too much but march around like those bullies in the schoolyard, only this time he's enjoying the abuse. This place could be called the 'Beat You Up and Take Your Lunch Money Club'. It's consensual so there cannot be any position for me to take beyond it's for me or it's not for me. I decide it's not for me. It's not my brave new world.

Someone else, I can't tell the gender through the rubber, is hanging by his or her feet from the ceiling. I check the rigging points out of habit. It looks like a pretty standard set-up. The human piñata spins on the rope.

'Slowly, very slowly, like two unhurried compass needles, the feet turn towards the right — north, north-east, east, south-east, south-south-west — then pause, and, after a few seconds, turn as unhurriedly back towards the left. South-south-west, south, southeast, east . . .'

'Drink?' I say.

Everyone nods yes in my general direction. I can't tell what anyone is thinking and don't look too closely because I really don't want to know.

I feel my way towards the bar in the dim light. I sit upon one of the stools. There is a man lying beneath my feet.

'Hello,' I say, deciding to be friendly.

'Hello.'

'So, what's your story?'

'Shoe fetish.'

'Really?'

'Yes.'

'How come?'

'The tough girls at school used to catch me and then stand on me and as it turns out . . . I like it.'

'You're kidding. That's how it started?'

'Think so.'

'Would you like me to stand on you?'

'Yes.'

'I can't hear you.' Now what am I doing, I wonder to myself.

'Yes, Mistress.'

Suddenly I'm a Mistress with a capital M.

'I know somewhere we could go,' he says hopefully.

'Not too far away, I hope.'

'No. It's a private room.'

I think, what the hell. It would seem rude to back out now.

'Lead the way.'

He leads me to a room to the side. It has low monkey bars.

'So you'll tell me what you want and how to do it, right?'

'Yes, Mistress.'

'So . . .'

'Hold onto the bars.'

I hold onto the bars. He lies on the ground.

'Now stand on my chest,' he says.

'Where?'

'Not on my heart.'

I gingerly place a boot on his chest, careful not to stand on his heart.

'Good Mistress, good. I can take more weight.'

I take some of the weight off my arms.

'Okay?'

'Yes, Mistress.' And his breathing changes. Happy breathing.

And so I walk around on him. Arms, legs, stomach, chest, lowering my weight carefully onto him using the monkey bars above for safety.

'Okay?'

'Oh, god, yes, Mistress.'

I reason to myself that this is a form of massage. I'm elongating the muscles not giving him a thrill. But . . . I'm giving him a thrill.

He begins to lick my boot. Oh dear.

'Thank you, Mistress, thank you.'

'That the lot then?' I say like a grocer.

'Yes, Mistress.'

I make my way back to my friends, drinks in hand. Again, nothing escapes the Duke.

'That took a long time,' he says. 'Where have you been?'

'I was . . . you know . . . walking around.'

'Oh yes.'

'On a guy.'

'Oh.'

'Yes.'

'So, how was it?'

'It was like standing on a guy. Did I just have sex? It didn't feel like sex. It just felt like . . . like . . . standing on soft ground.'

'It was sex to him.'

'Right.'

'Strange business, isn't it?'

We watch a man in tight leather skilfully tie a woman to a St Andrews Cross.

'Yes, it is strange.'

In the corner I can see the Prince on his knees with an expression on his face I've never seen before. The Junoesque dominatrix brings the riding crop down soundly on his back. I don't think he minds.

Luxey

The village of Luxey hides in a pine forest in the-middle-of-nowhere-France. The township is concealed in one of the largest industrial plantations in Europe. Rice, mulberry trees, tobacco and peanuts all failed here but the pine flourished. Well . . . after they drained the swamp the pine flourished.

In the old days, the people of Luxey fed their cattle through purpose-built windows from the kitchen straight into the barn while shepherds tended their flocks on stilts. This region was known as 'The French Sahara'. An inverse of the bright, dry desert, it was more a bleak marshy expanse. Hence the shepherds on stilts. One day the shepherds started to make up dances on their stilts. The first dance they made up is called 'The Stilt Users Quadrille'. Nowadays local stilt dancing groups – and there are twenty-one to choose from – are available for a modest fee.

We are here to perform at a music festival that literally takes over this tiny, old village. Continuous music from lunchtime until very late. The locals are very good about all this drunken frivolity. They let the party folk stay at their houses and don't complain about the noise.

We submit to the festival. It's muddy and joyous and

shines through the cracks of every part of this tiny, stone village. An enchanted village where there is always a party going on. We watch a French folk band. I'm sure I hear the word *fromage* in all of their songs. The French must really love their cheese.

We dance and laugh and, in the shabby hours of early morning, find a group of musicians taking it quietly by a fire in a nearby field. There are two Spanish guys, three Frenchmen and an Irishman cradling instruments in their arms.

'Come join us,' says the Irishman.

They take it in turns to play their music to the night sky.

The Spanish guys are Flamenco musicians. They play passionate gypsy music, full of drama, which cascades over us with infinite precision. Their wit astounds us. Diabolus in musica.

Then the French boys start up. One of them plays a mechanical violin with buttons. It drones and reveals hidden sympathetic strings.

The Irish guy sings a song in Gaelic. Simple, mysterious and moving.

'So?' The leader of the Spanish guys indicates in a single tiny sound that it is our turn to perform.

'Ah, we're not very musical. We're acrobats,' stammers the Duchess.

'The Prince could do a handstand for you,' I say foolishly.

The young men look confused. They look at each other. And then they look at us. We look at the ground.

Finally one of the French guys breaks the tension by sliding into a jaunty tune from the Middle Ages. The Irishman goes next and calls into being before us such a haunting melody on his violin that leaves us breathless. The Spanish dazzle us again with their fire and their brilliance once more.

And then they all turn and look at us. We look everywhere else.

The Duke rolls his eyes.

'Australians. I'll sing a song.'

The Duke grew up in New Zealand so he sings a Maori song. Damn New Zealanders with their treaties and their anti-nuclear policies and their first country in the world to give women the vote and they get to sing indigenous songs. I never learnt any Aboriginal songs when I grew up. But I did learn how to play 'God Save the Queen' on my recorder, which to this day, I remember how to do. Fortunately, no one seems to have a recorder.

The Duke's singing is lovely. The musicians pick up on something in his song and start improvising. An incredible fusion. The music comes to a triumphant end. We are left tingling and speechless with wonder.

And then they all turn and look at us. We huddle together a little.

'How about "Kookaburra Sits in the Old Gum Tree"?' says someone. I think it's the Duke.

I feel like I'm having an out of body experience. My god, no.

'Yes, sing us your kook kook song.'

This from the Spanish quarter. We have to participate. There's no way out. Decorum requires that we must sing this song and we must sing it now.

The Prince clears his throat and then the dirge begins. Stretched tight in an agony of embarrassment we all join in.

We sing the first lyric describing a bird in a tree and

I am already wondering if this song will ever be over.

The second line of the song asserts the cheerful disposition of the bird and his high status among the other wildlife as the Duchess shuffles her feet and Edmund looks decidedly unwell.

The third line of the song once again says that this is a very happy kookaburra and then leads into the big finish, which seems to indicate that the bird in question is homosexual.

The Duchess, Edmund and I stop singing. We thought that was the whole song. But it's not. The Lady and the Prince keep singing. It's an unholy duet. Something about gumdrops. I absently wonder what a gumdrop might be. Either way, the kookaburra eats them all and leaves none for the copyright holder of the song.

The Prince and the Lady finish in joyous rapture, lost in each other's eyes.

The horror of the tune hangs in the air between us.

'What's a kookaburra?' asks one of the French guys.

—

In the monochromatic light of just before proper dawn I walk down the cobblestone street in what I hope is the general direction of where I'm staying. I glance down a laneway and see what looks like the Prince and the Lady in an intimate embrace. By the time I've done my slow motion drunken double take, the couple have gone.

In a far-off field, I think I can see people dancing, dancing on stilts.

Nice

We are decorations at a rich man's wedding. Moving ornaments. Pretty, human baubles to adorn the marriage of a real prince and princess. These people are genuine royalty. Russian mafia royalty. Apparently Vladimir Putin is here but I can't see him. They bought us three times over, gave us a nice hotel and days off to lie on the beach so we can be warm tinsel for the happy event.

This particular wedding celebration has colonised a small peninsula of Nice for a week. Newly paved paths take you to numerous fully manufactured wonderlands that weren't there yesterday.

At the end of one of the paths, women are suspended in trees. Man-made rain falls onto them into a brand new pond below. More nymphs perform a kind of water ballet in the water.

At the end of another path there are horses doing tricks around a paddock accompanied by a brass band. Lithe young things jump on and off their backs as the animals race around the yard.

In the centre of the park there is a table where the guests will dine in the gentle dusk. A small battalion of waiters and girls dressed in food mill about.

Our job is to welcome the guests from on high as they walk through the gate. They've made us wear angel costumes to drift around in, secretly suspended on reasonably invisible ropes.

We smile, we sparkle, we garnish the door. I can see very young beautiful women on the arms of some spectacularly average-looking middle-aged men.

We have to stay up longer than usual. We have to stay up until after the guests have finished their dinner.

———

This particular piece of human trimming is starting to wilt. The fireworks have been going on for awhile. They go on and on. On and on and on. And on. And just when I think the fireworks have finished, they start up again. Edmund points to the car park. One of the vintage cars has caught fire. Big guys in tight suits run over to put out the blaze. The fire goes out and the party keeps going. Finally we get word that we are allowed to come down. We are hanging in the air like dead sheep. We weakly descend. We loll exhausted in the bus back to the hotel.

———

Next day we take it easy and stay close to water. We lounge around and order gin and tonics to match the pleasantly hot day.

'Would you like another one?' asks Edmund.

I stretch languidly.

'That would be lovely.'

'Monsieur, Monsieur. Two gin and tonics, *merci*.' And he clicks his fingers twice.

I inwardly cringe at the rudeness.

'Very good, sir,' says the waiter without a hint of annoyance at Edmund's manners.

'Also, Monsieur, what places are there of interest to see here in Nice?'

'Well, sir, there is La Promenade des Anglais or the Observatoire de Nice or even the Zone Pietonne, which is interesting if Sir would like to do some shopping.'

'Thank you, Monsieur, very helpful. That will be all.'

'Very good, Sir.'

'See that?' says Edmund. 'My French is getting really good. He understood every word I said. I could feel the love.'

'Edmund, you were just speaking English with a French accent.'

I write 'Having a nice time in Nice' on all of my postcards home. A shadow falls over the paper. I look up. A handsome man dressed mostly in a broad smile shades me from the sun.

'Would you mind if I sat here?'

'By all means.'

He gracefully tumbles into the lounge. He looks at me sideways from under long eyelashes and he runs his hands through his black hair. 'You know how some men buy really expensive cars to make up for certain, well, shortages? Well I don't even own a car. That's my bicycle over there.'

I take a sip of my drink. He shows me his white teeth. His muscles shift beneath his skin. Prometheus unrestrained. I have trouble pronouncing his name. He doesn't seem to mind.

Paris

Paris is not a city that you should see for the first time alone. It is a city to be shared with a friend, a lover or a companion. That's what it says in the in-flight magazine. My companion is somewhat untamed in the half-light and we don't see much of Paris outside of our hotel room. I still can't pronounce his name so I never use it.

My paramour with no name comes from Afghanistan. He is a big man with big hands and everything about him is big. He tells me never to go to Afghanistan. He is very serious about this.

'Not for a holiday, never. It is very dangerous there. I mean it,' he says, and holds my hands to emphasise his point.

I have to promise I will never go there and I do.

'So what's the veil all about?' I ask.

He takes a while before he answers.

'It is the eroticism of drawn curtains.'

He calls out in his sleep in his own language. He shouts to someone who is not in the room. He wakes himself up. He fucks like a poet. He tells me a story. A story from back home. When he was just a kid. The time when he had an automatic weapon aimed at his chest as he held a gun to the man's head. Some tiny slight in a public place had triggered the stand-off. Both of his cousins pulled their guns out but he told his cousins to put their guns away. He would handle it. His accent still has signs of the mountains in its tones.

'And we looked at each other, straight in the eye,' says the man with no name. 'The only thing we had to lose was our lives. It's the only thing we really have. You don't own your house or your car or your children. The only thing you really have to lose is your life. And we saw that in each other's eyes. And then he lowered his gun and I lowered mine. The man started laughing and said we could stay. Afterwards my cousins and I ran out into the snow and shot our guns into the night sky.'

He looks at our hands. 'Those cousins are dead now.'

And then we roll back into each other.

In the morning I have to go. He gives me a lift to the airport and, enfolded in his expansive chest, I listen to his heartbeat for a while before I go. I have to go. I have to . . .

I run through the traffic to the departure gates but all the jaywalking in the world won't hide the fact that I'm a tourist. And everybody hates a tourist.

Poznan

We fly to Poznan. A quick European flutter. Pretty much fly into the sky to fly straight back down again. Nowhere is very far from anywhere in Europe when travelling by plane. With all the mucking about in airports, I wonder if it wouldn't be better to take the train around here. I'd be happy lulled by a view and room to move about in and we wouldn't have to go through the interminable security screenings. But I do get a new teaspoon.

The Prince is late out of customs. Finally he trudges from the gates.

'What happened?' demands the Chancellor.

'I was stopped by customs. A dog came up and sat by me, so I patted it. I like dogs. But then a man in a big coat asked me to step this way. So I stepped this way. It was the drugs dog. He did a body search.' The Prince's voice cracks a little at this point. 'But this is the thing, I was standing there, touching my toes, when the custom officer says, "So, have you had a nice day?"'

—

Poland. Black birds against a grey canvas on this

summer's day, moody architecture against a saturnine sky and it's dusk.

Seven drummers lift into the air on pretty much a carnival ride with no safety bar. Dressed as military clown princes they hang by a thread from a crane. Mobile *homme*. A chandelier of men playing their trance-inducing litany; a complicated conversation between themselves involving shifting tempos of mathematical precision, flirting with their rhythms, playing with cadence. And then the percussive discussion becomes serious.

By degrees they become all form and no detail. Fade into silhouette. Cut-outs against the sky. They are so very high up. I'm a little afraid for them. They look fragile against the firmament. And then the fireworks go off. Europeans have no regard for fire safety. The band plays on. Backlit by exploding points of fire they finish arms outstretched.

It's the band from the airport.

—

We happen upon an outdoor café and order Zubrowka with apple juice. The drink is called Szarlotka and what with the Bison Grass from the Bialowieza Primeval Forest in it, it packs an almighty punch. It punches the Lady especially hard. She is openly throwing up in the street before too long. The Prince holds her hair back. We decide to deposit her in a taxi and send her home. The Duchess orders another round and sidles up to the Prince.

The Duke notices Edmund's shoes. 'Nice shoes, Edmund. Where'd you get them?'

'Nice.'

'Nice.'

'I found a special friend in Nice,' I confide. 'He fucked like a poet.'

'What, so you had really dirty sex and he hated himself afterwards?' says the Duke.

The conversation turns to accents. We all try to say 'Mary Had a Little Lamb' in accents from around the world. The worst of them is from Edmund whose accent begins in England, goes to Ireland, travels through South Africa and ends up in India where all bad accents go to die. He was trying to do a Brooklyn accent. The table erupts with mirth.

'That was awful,' says the Duke.

'It wasn't that bad,' says Edmund.

'No really, it was truly awful.'

'Just because New Zealanders are afraid of vowels.'

'Better than your flat accent, convict.'

And that's our cue to go home.

I stand up somewhat unsteadily. I hope I can remember how to walk.

'Well, now,' says the Duke. I follow his gaze to the end of the table. The Prince and the Duchess's faces are busy with each other. So are their hands.

'We'll let them find their own way home, shall we?' says the Duke.

———

The Lady looks positively haggard at breakfast.

'Those children wouldn't stop playing in the corridor last night. It was four in the morning. Who lets their kids play in the corridors until four in the morning?'

'I didn't hear any children,' yawns Edmund, 'but I'm on

the top floor. That guy pacing up and down in the room next to mine kept me up.'

The Duchess appears at the table.

'Morning,' she dispenses cheerily.

'Did you hear any children last night?' asks the Lady.

'Children? No, I slept like a baby,' says the Duchess, almost shyly.

The Duke leans forward.

'There is no one else at the hotel except for us, guys. They opened it just for the festival and just for us. The breakfast lady only comes in the morning to give us our regulation egg. She's gone by lunchtime. No one else is here at night except for us.'

The Lady is confused. 'But I heard children.'

The Prince bounds up. The Lady urgently takes him by the arm.

'Did you hear any children last night?'

'No. No children but I did see a woman in the room at the end. The door was open. She was sitting at the window.'

The Duke is all eyes. 'No one else is here.'

'The woman turned and looked at me,' says the Prince.

'No one here,' goggles the Duke.

'She said something that sounded like *Co robisz? To mój pokój*,' says the Prince.

Everyone loses the ability to move for a moment.

'Does anyone know any Polish?' asks the Lady.

We all look to the Duke in one smooth move. The Duke takes a deep breath.

'It means . . .' and he pauses for effect.

'Yes?' says the Lady impatiently.

'It's only an approximation.'

'Yes, yes?'

'It means . . .'

'Come on, come on.'

The Duke takes a breath. 'What do you think of me so far?'

The room falls into an unimpressed silence.

'No it doesn't,' says Edmund.

'Do you speak Polish?' asks the Lady in a faintly hysterical tone.

The Duke smiles. 'Not a word.'

———

The Lady is packed and sitting on the bus in ten minutes flat. Edmund is beside her soon after. The Prince soon after that. The rest of us climb aboard like we're escaping a natural disaster.

The Duke puts the bus into gear. The Lady points to the top floor.

'Is there a woman standing in that window?'

We all follow her outstretched arm.

There is a woman in a long white dress. She waves at us and then she turns to walk away. We all look again. Her elbows and knees are bending the wrong way. I think that's what I see. Is that what I see?

Someone screams. I think it's the Lady. The Duke puts his foot to the floor and the rest of us join in the screaming. We don't stop until we get to the airport.

Tinos

It is an outrage. We have to share rooms. A very nice family owns the hotel but they own a hotel that doesn't have enough rooms for us to have one to ourselves. This includes the very nice family. Some of them go and stay with relatives. The Prince, the Lady and the Duchess each have a real hotel room. They put the Duke and I in their lounge room, the Chancellor takes the children's bedroom and Edmund gets what could be the linen cupboard. The Generalissimo also has a room to himself, the shed out the back. The family tried to make it comfortable. He's really quite happy with the arrangement. So are we.

I leave my bags on the couch, borrow the family dog from the hotel and go for a walk along the beach. The dog is good company as I make my way along the shifting line marking sea from land. Not a breath of wind. I go for a quick swim. Make myself put my head under. The Aegean Sea is gentle against the skin and of the cleanest blue. The brilliant sun, the bleached buildings, the glass top sea, the hillside carved by thousands of years of western civilisation. There are glittering rocks along the shore beside the silver, luminescent sea. Kittens play in a garden and the nanny goats line up against the wall to escape the heat of the sun. In the distance I can see Edmund, on the shoreline, making an arch out of rocks.

Eventually I wind my way to the main street. The church, Panagio Evangelistria, is the centrepiece of the island. Pilgrims make their way from ferry to wharf to altar on hands and knees up the hill to the cathedral of mobiles. Articulating icons shift in the breeze and the priests sing hymns in the background.

—

I arrive back at the hotel. I return the dog with thanks to the very nice family and collapse on the balcony in one of the lounges. I breathe in the evening.

'Hey!'

The shout breaks the silence originating from seemingly nowhere.

'Hey there.'

I look behind me.

'Down here.'

I go over to the edge of the balcony and look down and there is the Prince standing below, one flight down. He leaps onto a low wall.

'Give us a hand.' And he extends his arm towards me.

'No worries,' I say in my best vernacular. I reach down and we hold hands. As a joke, I pretend to lift him onto the balcony. And then suddenly, I'm lifting him up to the balcony. He leaves the ground and then just keeps leaving it. Halfway to the landing he starts reaching for the railing and in a moment he's standing beside me. We are both very surprised. And then the Prince laughs the laugh that men use when I beat them at arm wrestles.

'Thanks for the lift.'

'Anytime,' I say, wiping my eyes. 'Since you're here, would you like refreshment?'

'Well, maybe one cheeky one.'

'You're a small-town boy, aren't you?' I say as I hand him a drink.

'I am.'

'You come from a big family, don't you?'

'Sure do. Eight of us. Five girls and three boys, including the steps. And we all look completely different. I have a sister with red hair and all my brothers have blond hair.' The Prince runs his hand through his impressively black hair. 'My dad was a Major in the Salvation Army until it was discovered he was fraternising with a soldier who wasn't his wife. He left the Salvos and Mum as well. Started a new family. Then he started another new one after that.'

'Can you play the trumpet?'

The Prince looks bashful for a moment. 'Yes, I can play the trumpet.'

'Did you play on street corners at Christmas?'

'I was made to.'

'Can you play "Stairway to Heaven" on the trumpet?'

'Yes. But just the first bit.'

'I'm suitably impressed.'

'You know what I reckon?'

'What?'

'When you've found the right way to breathe . . .'

'Yeah.'

'. . . then just breathe.' The Prince finishes his drink with a tip of his head. 'Better be off.'

'Need a hand?'

'No thanks.'

The Prince disappears, taking the stairs this time, as I settle back onto the lounge. A delicate breeze moves the branches of the trees. I take the Prince's advice and keep breathing.

The Duke appears at the top of the stairs. 'Good evening,' he says quietly.

'Good evening.' I raise my glass. 'Care to join me?'

The Duke settles on the other lounge and a companionable silence goes on longer than usual. I break the companionable silence.

'You seem a little maudlin this evening. Anything wrong?'

The Duke sighs. 'I miss Ivan, I miss London and I'm even missing the rain.'

'The rain that gets into your eyes?'

'Yes, even the rain that gets into your eyes.'

The Duke makes his way to his feet.

'I might go to bed.'

'Okay. 'Night.'

I can hear the sea in the distance rising and ebbing along the shore. Peaceful. I make my way indoors. The Duke has claimed the double bed and left the camp bed for me. Not a chivalrous sort, our Duke. Fortunately the camp bed is surprisingly comfortable. Oblivion is not hard to find tonight.

—

A sound wakes me. Still in half-dream I have to try to remember where I am. I feel like a blunt instrument. For a moment, I think I'm somewhere in Asia but then the word Europe echoes around my hollow head. The word Tinos follows shortly after. Then the loud sound again. It sounds like a banshee wailing in the night. Then another harridan joins the call. After a moment, a third voice. A young man's voice.

The Duke is sitting up with eyes like saucers. Without speaking we put on our shoes and hurry in the direction of the shrieking. It's coming from the Prince's room.

The Duchess and the Prince are in bed. The Prince is anxiously trying to be modest behind a sheet. The Duchess is howling at the Lady. The Lady is standing in the corner of the room and screaming something undecipherable back. And Edmund is there with his hair sticking up looking dishevelled.

'What happened?' demands the Duke.

'I don't know. I was asleep. I just followed the scream-ing,' says Edmund.

The Duke jumps into the fray with his best stentorian voice. 'Okay you two harpies, that is enough. They can hear you in Athens.'

The Lady whines something about he and she, he and me, and he and me and she . . .

'Stop snivelling,' snaps the Duchess. 'You are just a . . .' and then she calls the Lady a name. Not a very nice name. The room is very still for an extended moment. The Duchess has stepped over the line. The Lady col-lapses in on herself.

'You she-devil,' she manages through the sobbing.

Edmund leads her away keening quietly to herself. The Duke rounds on the Prince.

'Stop sleeping with the women in the company, okay?'

The Prince tries on his cutest smile. It has absolutely no effect on the Duke.

'No, I'm serious. Just stop it.'

The Prince finds the decency to look shamefaced.

—

We wake to a crazy wind. The meltemi wind. A strong, dry wind from the north. The trees must be exhausted. The sea is as much white as blue and the horizon is a soft-edged, ghostly blur. Someone's god is angry and no one is listening.

—

It is very, very tense at breakfast. The Duchess and the Lady perform elaborate choreographies to avoid each other at the morning table, it is deathly quiet in the bus and warm-up is a sullen affair. We have a show to do. It doesn't seem likely but we have to go through the rigmarole of getting ready anyway. We dress and stand ready, waiting for the call one way or another. And then the wind dies off suddenly.

We're on. We walk down to the site. The music begins. We climb. The wind picks up a little. The lights snap on. The audience looks up.

Six figures are caught in the glare. The Duke, the Duchess, the Lady, the Prince, the Courtesan and Edmund stand on small planets floating in the air.

The Prince walks out onto a tightrope. It's not fixed to anything at the other end. He feeds the rope out through his hands and places his foot upon it. With each footfall the rope becomes taut and he is suspended in mid-air, stepping into the nothingness – feeding the rope out into the darkness.

A gust of wind gets under the wire and the Prince crouches against it. There are a delicate couple of moments, and then he straightens, takes another step and is plunged into darkness.

'What happened to the lights?' I shout into the night.

'The Prince is in trouble,' hisses the Duke.

'Can the Generalissimo see? Does he know?'

We look down and try to see where our 'Safety Officer' is standing. He's not in the usual place. The Prince is tangled in the rigging. He is buffeted by the wind. The show can't go on. We need the Generalissimo to call the show off.

'Where is that stupid little man?' bellows the Duke.

We desperately search the ground. Finally the Duke sees the Generalissimo off to the side smoking a cigarette and listening to his iPod. We call out to him. The Duke calls him many things. Some things I've never heard before. We wave our arms around. The Generalissimo plays air drums along to the music. I look around for something to throw.

My hand finds a water bottle. I aim for his head. Luckily for me it falls short and lands at the Generalissimo's feet. He looks up. We point out the Prince's predicament largely in dumb show. The Generalissimo stubs out his cigarette. He makes the sign to stop the show to the Chancellor. The announcement to the audience is made over the loudspeaker: 'We are sorry but due to technical problems, we will have to end tonight's performance.'

The Prince is still struggling to work out the knot he is now part of, as the Duke begins to scale the steel structure. He shins up to the joist and begins to precariously climb along the truss. The Prince is being whipped about like a flag in the wind.

The Duke makes his way in slow motion along the buttress, leaning into the gale. The wind blows his hair into his eyes. He makes it to the beam the Prince is hanging from when a sudden squall knocks him sideways. As he falls he reaches out to the truss and miraculously arrests his plummet to the ground. He holds on by fingertips, somehow withstanding a series of flurries. When they have subsided, somewhat, he swings like a child on monkey bars beneath the steel beam towards the Prince. The Prince is whipped like washing flapping on a clothesline.

When the Duke reaches the Prince, he uses what must be superhuman strength to clamber back up onto the steel support. He carefully unwinds the frightened kid and helps him up to the relative safety of the beam. They slowly, painfully slowly, come down. As they descend they narrowly avoid being dashed into the ground by random blasts from the storm. When the Prince finally reaches terra firma, he holds the earth, embraces the ground. I think there may be some kissing going on.

The Generalissimo comes up to the Prince 'all jovial like' and plants a hand on his back.

'No harm, then?'

The Prince shrugs off the offending paw. 'Fuck off, man.'

There is the promise of real violence in his eyes. After a tense moment, the Prince stalks off to the dressing room. The Duchess and the Lady eye each other off for comforting rights but then both hurry off after the Prince. The Duke faces the Generalissimo.

'I don't want to hear it, faggot.' And with that, the Generalissimo sets off in the opposite direction.

I look at the Duke and something in his aspect makes me feel suddenly very nervous about the Generalissimo's future health.

—

On the way back to the hotel we spot the Generalissimo walking down a pier, swaying in the gale. Or maybe he is just really, really drunk.

Rome

All roads lead to Rome and apparently they do because here I am on a plane making its descent into Fiumicino Airport. We have a week off before we have to start work again and I've come straight to Rome. The Duke has ducked back to London to see his boyfriend, the Duchess has gone to Berlin, Edmund and the Prince have gone to Croatia – they have heard all the women there are beautiful – and the Lady stayed on in Tinos for reasons known only to herself. The Chancellor went back to Ghent to talk to the agent and I don't care where the Generalissimo went.

As we taxi along the runway I see lost bags sitting untidily in the middle of the tarmac. At baggage claim, there are more bags in piles in lost luggage than on the carousel. This must be where old bags come to die. I anxiously wait for my own to appear from the hole in the wall. I'm one of the lucky ones. Other passengers stand unkempt and disappointed, looking forward to spending the next couple of days in the clothes they are wearing. Among the ranks of the unlucky, the reappearing band is there, standing in the ranks of the rumpled. The guy who caught my phone sees me. I consider winking. I decide against it. We almost acknowledge each other but we don't. I manhandle my luggage off the conveyer belt and look for the exit.

———

From my room I see a man eating an orange from a window in the opposite building, three storeys up, enjoying the dusk. I enjoy him enjoying the dusk.

It's a comely day with a subversive sun struggling through the clouds and it's raining and I realise that's what I miss. I miss the rain. It's not much of a sunset but the air is warm and the rain is warm, warm rain, and now I've washed my things I enjoy the simple pleasure of hanging clothes on the balcony. I take refuge in the banal and the domestic and spend my first night in Rome quietly. I have some time here before the rest of them turn up. I sort through my suitcase. The travel ritual. I unpack everything from my bag. I sort and fold and smooth and descend into the meditation of reorganisation. When living out of a suitcase I feel as righteous as a Spartan. I admire new memories in trinket form and spend time alone expensively granted on a green and pink bedspread. My maps are unfolded but, as yet, unread. I'm in Rome. That's all I need to know tonight.

———

Metrobus Roma. It's a hot day and a loud American voice is taking up all the space in the bus. I feel for the locals. Two thousand years of tourists must get to be a bit much. Everyone wears bare arms, floral dresses and high heels on the scooters just like they do in the movies.

I try not to picture what it would be like if they came off all the while secretly wishing I had the courage to ride a motorbike in light cotton and strappy sandals.

—

I'm having a charming dinner in a charming restaurant in a charming side street when two angry voices disturb the charm of the evening. Something has happened between two scooters in the traffic and they've stopped to talk about it in very loud voices and raised fists. Two men and a woman. One of the men throws a punch and the woman starts screaming. She screams in that high-pitched hysterical sound common in women all around the world when a fight is getting out of control. The sound of domestics and pub brawls. Or in this case, when a man hits your boyfriend with his motorbike helmet. My waiter runs over and breaks up the fight and we all go back to our charming dinners.

—

When in Rome, you go to the Vatican. The attendants slouch about in all the various aspects of boredom. Artefacts themselves buried alive in an opulent palace. One of them breathes one of the greatest sighs I have ever heard.

I get to the roof and I find a post office. Delighted, I buy postcards from the smallest country in the world. I hear a voice behind me.

'Long time no see.'

That voice. The way the speaker bears down upon the throat to produce a voice that scrapes into the ear.

Infantile, nasal and upwardly inflected. That ghastly sound. The Princess.

'Thought I'd see you here. Yes. I heard the show was coming to Rome. I'm a guide here now. Would you like some company? I can give you a guided tour.'

'God no.'

'Beg your pardon?'

'Of course, Princess.'

'I'll charge you mate's rates.'

'I have to pay you?'

'A girl's got to make a living.'

'You've made friends since you moved here?'

'Oh yes. Making friends is easy. Remembering their names is hard.'

The delights of visiting a museum with a princess

There are none.

A short tour of
the Vatican

Not in the right frame of mind for martyred young men or endless pictures of mothers with infants, we head towards the ancients. We find ourselves in the Gregorian Egyptian Museum. There is a mummy in the corner. It lies behind glass. It is genuinely creepy. The Princess decides to tell me all about it.

'The inhabitants of ancient Egypt were called mummies. They lived in the Sarah Desert. Mummies are wrapped in bandages so they don't hurt themselves in the afterlife.'

—

Standing before the Incendio di Borgo the Princess tells me, 'Pope Leo extinguished a fire with the sign of the cross. He had powerful gestures. You stepped out of the way if he waved at you.'

—

At *Meeting of St Leo the Great with Attila, King of the*

Huns, she says, 'The two men flying in this painting depict early representations of modern day superheroes.'

—

Now we are standing in front of The Belvedere Torso. Words can't describe . . . well, apparently they can. The Princess has a go.

'This is a body with no arms, no legs and no head. I think you will also notice that he is missing his . . .'

And at this point she looks at the statue's lap and whistles twice.

—

At *Adam and Eve in the Garden of Eden*, the Princess says 'The first book of the bible is Genius. This is a history book. Adam and Eve were banished from Eden for eating all the apples and not wearing any clothes.'

I can't stand it any longer. 'Please stop talking.'

'But I was just telling you . . .'

'No really. Stop talking.'

'Yes, but . . .'

'Stop talking.'

She opens her mouth.

'Stop talking.'

She closes her mouth. It's a miracle at St Peters. She actually stops talking.

But then we get to the Sistine Chapel. There is a sign that says 'Talking is Prohibited' in the Sistine Chapel. This is because people insist upon talking in the Sistine Chapel. There are men standing around and their only job is to shush people in order to remind them that you mustn't talk in the Sistine Chapel. They are working flat out. And what are these people saying?

'Awesome.'

'Yeah, awesome.'

'Isn't it awesome?'

'Awesome.'

And then the miracle is undone. The Princess begins talking again. She says, sotto voce, 'Saul was called Paul after he contorted to Christianity.'

The Guard goes shush.

'He preached holy acrimony, which is another name for marriage.'

The Guard goes shush again.

'The heathens did not believe in Paul, so he got stoned.'

'SHUSH!'

—

We reach the staircase that takes us back into the world. The descent back into sinfulness once more. When we are outside, I run away from the Princess. I don't make excuses. I just duck down a side street and run away.

I run past the guy who caught my phone at the airport. He's running in the opposite direction. There is a moment of astonished recognition between us before I am at the next corner and he's out of sight.

The Anagram of
Banach-Tarski

When in Rome, as in Paris, it would seem one needs a companion. Just not any companion. I sit down in a park – probably a bloody significant park – and feel the leaden weight of loneliness.

I reach out for the nearest tourist at a café. A man with black-rimmed glasses and amusing hair sits at the next table from me. Suddenly the world is delightful again.

We are on a platform at the Stazione Centrale Roma and a cheerful one-hit wonder plays through a loud speaker.

'All the best songs in the world are one-hit wonders,' I say.

'I concur.'

He has a room at Oxford. His field is pure mathematics. He is genuinely brilliant. Definitely on the spectrum. This makes him a great tour guide. And he has a sense of humour. A sense of humour that needs years of study to grasp.

'Do mathematicians tell each other jokes?' I ask.

'They do.'

'Tell me one.'

'What's the anagram of Banach-Tarski?'

'I don't know, what is an anagram of Banach-Tarski?'

'Banach-Tarski, Banach-Tarski.' And he smiles beautifully.

'You knew I wouldn't get it.'

'Yes, I knew that.'

'So, why's it funny?'

'Well, Banach-Tarski is a theory whereby a sphere can be cut into a finite set of pieces and then when you put the sphere put back together, it's twice its size.'

'I'm going to Newgrange for the winter solstice.'

'Did you know that the construction of the tomb at Newgrange would have taken a workforce of three hundred at least twenty years?'

'I didn't know that.'

'Furthermore, the famous triple spiral on the standing stone in the central recess of the chamber actually consists of a total of six spirals.'

'Really?'

'I'll show you.'

He traces the shape on my leg. I lose count of the spirals.

And then he says that he senses I am sad. And, suddenly, I am.

'Everything's so uncertain,' I say. 'I'm not so young anymore. Maybe I finally need some certainty.'

'The uncertainty principal is a fundamental, inescapable property of the world.'

'That story about the grasshopper and the . . . I can never remember the other animal. Tortoise?'

'An ant, grasshopper.'

Colosseo

I find the site easily enough. It's across the road from the Coliseum. The Chancellor is talking to the sound guy. The Lady is setting up her gear beside a road case. I decide to join the Lady.

'How was Tinos?'

'I didn't stay in Tinos. I jumped on a ferry and went to Mykonos and partied on the beach. It was great. I got an all-over tan. All over.'

She looks like she might have spent a little too long on the beach. She radiates heat and discomfort. She's in pain.

'I see you got a bit of colour.'

'By tomorrow it will have faded into a beautiful golden brown,' she says.

I hope for her sake that it does.

Edmund and the Prince walk up.

'Morning ladies,' says the Prince.

'So, did you have a suitably debauched time in Croatia?' I ask.

'Were the women beautiful?' asks the Lady.

'What happens in Croatia, stays in Croatia,' says Edmund.

'I bet you nothing happened,' says the Lady.

'Nothing did happen,' says the Prince. 'We just couldn't make it happen. Either of us.'

'But were the women beautiful?' asks the Lady.

Edmund looks genuinely sad. 'Yeah, the women were beautiful.'

'Made it all the worse,' says the Prince.

Someone is shouting. The Lady stiffens. We all look across the street and there is the Duchess wearing towering platform heels and a bright dress made out of doilies. She is waving at us. We all wave back. She moons us. Then she runs through the traffic to join the mildly horrified group.

'Berlin was amazing,' she says, after miraculously surviving the traffic. 'I love it, I love it, I love it. I met all of these amazing artists and made all of these amazing connections and had all of this amazing sex and it was just . . .'

'Amazing?' says Edmund.

'Yeah.'

'You do look well,' says a baritone voice behind us. It's the Duke.

The Duchess falls into him with what can only be described as a squeal. 'How was London?'

'Moments away from complete anarchy.' He clasps his hands and smiles like a schoolteacher. 'You all look well rested.' We don't, but we all nod in friendly agreement. 'Show's at eight so we'd better get to it.'

'I feel like someone's missing,' says Edmund.

'Everyone's here,' says the Duchess.

The Chancellor does her impersonation of running up to us. It's like running but slower.

'The Generalissimo has missed his flight,' she says when she finally reaches us.

'Missed his flight?' repeats the Duchess.

'Missed his flight,' confirms the Chancellor.

'When can he get here?' demands the Duke.

'Tomorrow morning,' says the Chancellor in a small voice.

'Tomorrow morning?' we all thunder back pretty much in unison.

'Where the hell is he?' asks the Duke.

'He's stuck in Mexico.'

'Why in God's name would you go all the way to Mexico with less than a week off?'

'Cheap cocaine?' says Edmund.

The Duke harrumphs and paces in a quick circle. By the time he's come back round the corner he's got his game face on.

'Okay. Okay. Okay. We can put the rig up without him. I'll come back when it's done and then all of you need to check your equipment at least three times and find a buddy to check it after you. Okay?'

We nod in fear as much as in agreement.

'Well?' the Duke glares at us.

We all turn our attention to the material world and start looking for our gear.

—

The sky is a very particular shade of blue in this part of the world and it illuminates the Flavian Amphitheatre just so. Even the moon comes out to adorn the event. We are written in a trick of the light and an impressive view. We are in the otherworld. We are in the postcard.

'That was amazing,' says the Duchess.

The Prince does one of his more muscular handstands to mark the occasion.

The charms of travelling on minibuses

There are none.

The road to hell
is paved with good
intentions but you get
there in a minibus

Hours yet until the final destination. Clean every-thing promises relief at the end of a bus ride that feels like it has been going on now for the better part of a week when we've actually only been in the bus for five hours. Five long, boring, cramped hours.

The Prince and his small harem are silent. The two women have put invisibility spells on each other. The spells kind of work. At least they can't see each other.

The Chancellor is driving and Edmund is her hapless navigator. The Chancellor insists on playing the Beatles over and over again. She has decided that the driver chooses the music. 'She loves you, yeah, yeah, yeah' drones on and on and on. Finally she changes the music. At last. And then she puts on The Wiggles and sings along. I think it is the happiest I have ever seen her. This may be as miserable as I have ever been.

An opulent tour bus overtakes us. It's the band from the airport travelling in a hotel on wheels. I can see beds, a bar, a bathroom and a small kitchen. One guy is watching TV in his mobile castle. A couple of them play cards and another guy is asleep in a bunk bed. And then I see the guy who caught my phone. He's reading a book on what looks like a very comfortable lounge. He looks up and our eyes meet, briefly. Their bus effortlessly pulls away.

'*Ausgang* must be a very large city,' says the Lady. 'That's the tenth sign I've seen. All roads seem to lead to *Ausgang*.'

'*Ausgang* means exit,' says the Chancellor through gritted teeth.

Edmund calls out the directions.

'Take the exit toward A1/E45, keep left at the fork, follow the signs for Firenze/E45/A1 and merge onto A1/E45, Take the exit onto A11/E76 toward E89/Livorno/A12/Pisa Nord/Genova and it's a partial toll road. Take the exit toward Lucca Ovest/E80/A12/Genova/Viareggio. It's a toll road. Merge onto A11. It's a toll road. Take the exit onto A12 toward Livorno/Genova, which are toll roads and then take the exit Genova Est and continue down the toll road. Make a slight right toward Via Bobbio, a slight left at Via Bobbio and then turn right at Via Bobbio/SS45.'

We pull into La Spezia. We're lost.

'I knew we shouldn't be heading west,' explodes the Chancellor.

'We should have taken the exit Genova Est not the A15 toward La Spezia. That's where we went wrong,' says the Duke after scrutinising the map.

'I'm sure I said that,' says Edmund.

'You did not,' says the Chancellor.

'I did.'

'Did not.'

'DID!'

'Look, whatever,' says the Duke. 'The mistake's been made. No reason to point fingers now. Let's just get back on the road.'

'Can't we just stop for a quick beer at that bar over there,' asks the Generalissimo, clearly not grasping the dangerous mood of the company.

'NO,' everyone choruses, about one degree from white rage.

We all squeeze back into the minibus. The Chancellor, in a great temper, puts her foot on the accelerator before the door has been slammed shut and proceeds to hit a pedestrian with the side mirror of the van. The Duchess jumps out to investigate and make amends.

'THAT WAS YOUR FAULT, EDMUND,' screams the Chancellor.

'How can that be my fault?'

'You . . . are . . . the . . . navigator.'

'So that means I have to say things like watch out for that car, watch out for that traffic light and watch out for every single person that walks near the car? Doesn't the driver take some responsibility for not running into things?'

'No. You are the navigator. You have to navigate.'

Edmund fumes back at her. He says something under his breath.

The Duke steps in. 'Hang on, you two. Look, I'll drive and the Lady can navigate.'

'Must I?' The Lady doesn't want to leave the Prince with the Duchess.

I offer myself up. 'I will.'

'Okay,' says the Duke as he snatches the map from Edmund's hands.

The Duchess returns to the van.

'The man was very good about it. He said he wasn't hurt and just went on his way. He did look a bit put out.'

The Chancellor glowers at Edmund. 'That's lucky for you.'

Edmund scowls back. 'Lucky for you, you mean.'

'No, I mean lucky for you.'

'You mean lucky for you.'

The Duke cuts in with his best dad voice. 'I swear if you two don't fucking well shut up, I'm leaving you on the side of the road and driving off.'

'Sounds fine to me,' says Edmund and then quickly decides against saying any more as he catches the warning in the Duke's eyes.

—

The Duke is driving like a man possessed by a demon. A demon with a very foul mouth.

'Fuck you, you fucking fuck,' says the Duke, directing his very worst manners towards a very small red Fiat.

'Fuck's such a flexible word used in this example as a verb, an adjective and a noun,' quips Edmund with more courage than sense.

'Cunt!' bellows the Duke. 'Cunt, cunt, cunt, fucking cunt.'

'And the award for the most gratuitous use of the word cunt in a minivan goes to . . . '

I really don't think Edmund is grasping the situation.

The Duke pulls the minibus up by the side of the road.

'That's it. Get out.'

Edmund half-smiles.

'What?'

'Get out.'

The Duke reaches over and opens the door.

'Out!'

Edmund looks foolishly at the open door. Kind of smiling.

'OUT!'

Edmund gets out of the van. The Duke slams the door after him and drives away.

A desolate looking Edmund recedes into the distance. He even kicks a pebble forlornly.

'You are not going to leave him there, are you?' the Chancellor asks. 'We need him for the show.'

The Duke says nothing for a long time. No one dares to say anything for a good time after that. Eventually the Duke does a greatly illegal u-turn and heads back to get Edmund.

Genova

The restaurant has a nice aspect and the horizon is dressed its prettiest pinks, its most feminine clouds. But most importantly, we are no longer sitting in a mini-bus anymore. The Prince does a handstand in the street to assert the fact that we are not in a minibus anymore.

'Italian men give me lovely high blood pressure,' says the Duke, watching a particularly fine specimen strut down the street.

The waiter appears, ready to take our orders.

'*Buongiorno.*'

'*Buongiorno*,' we chorus back.

The waiter places the menus on the table.

'*Preghiamo,*' says Edmund, with his best manners in place.

'You're suddenly very devout,' says the Duke.

'What did I say?'

'Let us pray.'

'What is it supposed to be?'

'*Prego.*'

'*Prego. Ciao.*'

'What did you say?'

'*Ciao.* You know, thank you.'

'You know . . .'

'What?'

'Doesn't matter.'

'*Senza cane*,' says the Lady, pointing to the menu.

'*Un bel cazzone*,' says Edmund, reading carefully.

The waiter reveals the fact that he speaks English.

'I think you want *senza carne*, without meat,' he says to the Lady as he raises his well-kept eyebrow. 'I can assure you we do not serve dog at this restaurant. And you, sir, 'I hope you mean *un bel calzone*. *Un bel cazzone* is a male private part.'

The rest of us point to the dishes we want on the menu. No one attempts to pronounce anything anymore.

'Anything to drink?'

'Eight lattes please,' says Edmund.

'Hot or cold?'

'Oh, hot.'

Ten minutes later eight hot glasses of milk come to the table.

'Your lattes,' says the waiter as he places them on the table with a flourish.

'I'm sick of fine dining,' says Edmund.

Bassano

An orange aperitif sits before me on wooden table somewhere in Bassano. It's six in the evening or thereabouts. Another gorgeous old town tossed clumsily together on the peak of a small hill. The jewellery moon from this afternoon now emanates in the rich sky above the graceful curves of the hills.

The Duke downs his grappa in a single gesture.

'This is the never-ending tour. I wish I didn't have to spend my time screaming "You fucking lazy cunt" at the Generalissimo every bump in and out.'

'I can't believe what happened in Rome. Did you tell the Office?'

'They say they'll deal with it when we get back and, anyway, they say it's too expensive to replace him.'

'That's no good.'

'Nothing we can do.'

'We could check out the old town.'

'Check out another old town for something completely different,' says the Duke.

We gather up the Prince, the Duchess, the Lady and Edmund after dinner and start scouring the streets for a distracting little bar. We find one. It is packed wall to wall with astonishing young models. Edmund and the

Prince pretty much sprint over to the young girls. They don't even pretend to be casual about it.

We were brought to Bassano by a famous fashion label. The event was very well organised. Apparently Naomi Campbell is here but I can't see her. I'm surprised to find that the faces of the models are no more beautiful than any other girl in their late teenage years. I expected such beauty that I would have to avert my eyes but no, apparently it's all in the make-up and stylists. They sit around in their expensive hair and nails. I crouch in another corner wearing my cheap teeth and flat shoes trying not to notice the lack of attention I'm commanding.

—

In no time at all, the Prince is making a gaggle of gangly girls giggle at the bar. A handstand may have been involved. The Duchess and the Lady don't look very happy. Their discontent and a few glasses of wine bring them closer together.

'He's a bastard!' says the Lady.

'Such a bastard,' agrees the Duchess.

'A great big bastardly bastard,' slurs the Lady. She's had a bit to drink.

'Bastard.'

'He's a scoundrel,' says the Duke.

'A villain,' I say.

The Duke and I don't care either way. We like the Prince, but this is fun.

'A rogue,' asserts the Duke.

'A thorough rascal,' I add.

'A scallywag, even,' says the Duke reaching for his old words.

'Why sir, a damned scamp.' I'm happy with that one.

The Duchess makes it to her feet and weaves her way over to the Prince.

'You sir, are a cad and a bounder.'

We applaud her wit from our table.

'Oh, very good,' says the Duke.

The Prince gets a faraway look in his eyes and the girls titter nervously.

The Duchess is righteous. The Duchess is noble. The Duchess is upstanding.

'Come, Lady. Let us leave this miscreant, good-for-nothing lowlife to his floosies.'

This elicits another warm round of applause from the table.

The Duke lifts his glass. 'Good show.'

The two women sweep off, gathering their moral high ground around themselves like cloaks and become best friends forever. At least the Prince is finally off the hook. I see him later ensconced between two young lovelies having the time of his life. I don't think he minds.

—

A young designer insists on buying me a drink. He looks deeply concerned.

'I'm concerned,' he says. 'I mean, we could hit it off really well, end up having a few more drinks, next thing you know we could go for a walk along one of these romantic streets, I could invite you back to my room, we could have an incredible time together and really make a very unique connection. Then we go out a few more times, get to know each other's friends, decide to take our relationship to the next level . . .'

'I'm leaving town in the morning,' I say.

'Can I buy you another drink?'

He's fun. He's handsome. He has very broad and muscular shoulders. He's a doe-eyed predator living the good life while he can. And sometimes you want to get caught.

His hotel room is much nicer than mine. But the thing is, it's a twin share and his roommate is already in flagrante delicto with one of the models from the show.

The young designer apologises for there not being much room in Europe and so, not wanting to make a fuss, I find myself in a strange duet with the couple on the other bed. Our voices harmonise and fill the room. No one seems to mind.

—

At ten in the morning I find myself blinking into a far too bright morning at the entrance to a hotel I have little recollection of ever seeing before. I have absolutely no idea where I am. I reach back into the night before and dimly recall a taxi ride. I walk to the corner of the street. A sign says Fabriano. I think it is the next town over from Bassano. The company leaves Bassano in an hour. I'm in Fabriano. I need to find a coffee and a taxi. The coffee part is easy. The taxi bit isn't working out so well. I keep walking in what I hope is the general direction of Bassano. I suppose I'll eventually get there if I walk. Eventually.

I walk and walk and then walk some more until finally I pause to entreat the universe, arms outstretched, 'Come on. You know I'm a good person.' And then I pause. Not entirely true.

I reach the edge of town and like a vision, a taxi

appears in the distance. I flag it down. I feel like a crazy woman. I certainly must look like a crazy woman.

'Bassano?'

'No, no . . .' and then the driver says a lot of stuff in Italian.

'Please, please you have to take me *per favore, per favore.*'

He says some numbers in Italian. I recognise the word for eight. He writes the numbers on a piece of paper. Big numbers that represent a lot of money.

'I can't afford that.'

He begins to drive away.

'Look, look, this is all I've got.'

He doesn't look pleased. I consider tears. He nods his head shortly. I leap into the taxi. This is going to be the most expensive ride of my life.

———

We finally reach the hotel. I can see the others coming down to the foyer with their bags. I avoid being seen by the Chancellor and sprint to the lifts. I open the door of my room and stumble inside. For a moment, I can't cope. I really can't cope. And then I can cope again. I toss my things into my bag with wild abandon. I take a shower only long enough to get good and damp and walk through a cloud of perfume. I dash to the lift.

The elevator doors open to an empty foyer. The foyer is deserted. There is not even anyone at the counter. They've left me. I walk slowly towards the front doors. I can't believe they left me. I put down my bag. I've been abandoned. Tossed aside. Renounced. Relinquished. Done away with, dispensed with, thrown over, disowned, disavowed, discarded, set aside, left high and dry, left in the lurch, left stranded, given up, forsaken and abjured. And I'm only ten minutes late. I look around for a chair in which to weep.

And then I hear the Duke's voice. And the laughter. It's coming from the restaurant. I follow the sound of the laughter and there they all are, having breakfast together. They all seem to be replaying a very involved prattfall from the Duke. He's the one who sees me first.

'Morning, Sunshine.'

'Aren't we supposed to be on the road by now?'

'No. We leave at one. Coffee?'

'Yes. Coffee.'

I take my place in the pack.

Stresa

It's time for another of the Duke's sly holidays on the side. He engineers a way for us to spend the weekend at Stresa. We stay at the Hotel Du Parc. It has a delicate charm and a view of the lake. I decide I could live here.

We meet in the foyer to go swimming. The Duke, Edmund and the Duchess appear with towels in hand. The Duchess is already in her bikini. We set off down the hill.

Halfway down the hill, some English tourists materialise. We are out of our heads with tension and maybe a little bored with each other. We have to bring some new people on tour and three English tourists decide to manifest themselves halfway down a street. The Duke, Duchess and Edmund have heard things on the wind and are now possessed with the ghosts of Christmas vaudeville. They are enchanted.

'Hello. My name is Paulie. I come from Flimby and I do like to keep in mediocre physical shape,' says the Duke.

'Hi, my name is Suzie and I come from Bonkle. Shall we perform an indecent act?' says the Duchess.

'Good afternoon. My name is Dicky and I come from the Aird of Sleat,' says Edmund as he relieves himself on a local monument.

I decide to take my new friends to dinner.

'My lobster's too big,' says Paulie. 'More wine?'

'Yes thank you,' says Dicky. 'I like to be good and drunk on holiday.'

'Yes, I love to dress up and then hang out in the gutter in my own vomit,' says Suzie.

'We all like to do that,' says Paulie.

We laugh until we cry. We can't move. We dissolve into making faces at each other. It's a mania. The joke's not even that funny anymore.

We swim in the lake. It is cold and peaceful and we are quiet together for a moment. Everyone is beautiful.

Chieri

Edmund is disappointed by the show. They think he doesn't care but he does. I try to smooth over his disappointment by making it someone else's fault. None of us was very good tonight. The cracks are beginning to show.

Everyone's tired. Everyone's slow. Everyone's at least a little bit injured. The Generalissimo orders whisky with beer chasers all through dinner. Anyone with any sense leaves early. The Lady corners me before I can join the ranks of anyone with any sense. She puts a drink in front of me.

'For you.'

I know that look. She's going to tell me another story. The Duke and the Generalissimo have started to raise their voices at each other in the background.

'Did you ever have any pets?' she purrs.

'Ah, yeah. I had a little dog when I was growing up. Did you?'

'I had a kitten once.'

'That's nice.'

'I called him Socks. He had four white paws that looked like socks. So that's why I called him Socks.'

'Right.'

At the next table I can hear the Duke.

'There is no excuse for what happened in Tinos.'

The Generalissimo matches the Duke's tone. 'That wasn't my fault.'

The Lady moves her face very close to mine.

'And I had this big, big ornate mirror. It was very big and very heavy and it was painted gold. Anyway, one day Socks was playing in front of the mirror.'

'I don't think I want to hear this.'

'So cute with his little toy . . . he didn't notice the mirror begin to fall . . .'

'I really don't want to hear this.'

'It made such a terrible noise when it landed.'

'Please don't go on.'

'The mirror cut off Sock's head.'

She goes on. I put my head in my hands.

'It took a couple of minutes for the meowing to stop.' She puts a hand on my arm. 'What was your little dog called?'

The Duke and the Generalissimo are starting to put their hands in each other's faces.

'Incompetent,' the Duke spits at the Generalissimo.

'Arrogant,' bellows the Generalissimo.

'Drunken moron.'

'You're a drunken moron.'

'Oh, go fuck yourself.'

'You go fuck yourself.'

'You go fuck yourself.'

'You go fuck yourself.'

The Duke finally breaks the witless exchange. 'You are a little, little man.'

The Generalissimo looks ready to start throwing tables about.

I take the Duke by the arm. 'Let's go.'

The Duke tosses invisible hair. 'Yes, let's.'

The Generalissimo turns his fury upon me. 'And you, you are a bitch.'

Only he doesn't say 'bitch', he says the word like he's a gangster or a highly paid recording artist. He pronounces it 'biatch'. It looks like he enjoys saying it. And then he adds the gesture. He 'flips me the bird' inches from my face. His big, misshapen hand smells faintly of cigarettes and something I try hard not to identify. His extended middle finger doesn't look a bird. And 'flip'? Raise is probably closer. It is nevertheless an obnoxious gesture in close proximity to my head. He continues to say 'biatch' over and over again. Working the vowel sounds he moves into a falling minor third, the first interval a child learns. Never the one for wit, our Generalissimo.

The Duke shifts his stance and I feel sure that if this gets ugly, I can always throw the Duke at the Generalissimo in the way one would throw a Rottweiler at an intruder. The Duke knows violence in a way I never want to understand. The Generalissimo's large, dirty fist remains in my face. He continues to incant his single insult. I decide I'm not going to retaliate. I'm not going to meet him at his dumb level. I'm going to just stand here and take it.

'Biatch, biatch, biatch, biatch,' sings the Generalissimo to the tune of 'Bye Baby Bunting'. Damn that taunting, falling minor third.

I lose my temper after all and move without thinking. I slice his hand out of my face so quickly it takes the Generalissimo a moment to realise his arm is back at his side. He's very drunk and loses balance slightly. His small loss of equilibrium turns into a marionette's stumble into a nearby chair. This is followed by an awkward tumble onto the floor, at which point the chair falls on top of him.

Wordlessly, the Duke and I decide upon a hasty retreat. We find the truck parked a couple of streets away and the Duke drives it slowly out of the square.

'Quite the rapper, our Generalissimo,' says the Duke. 'I had to resist the urge to kick him when he fell down. Does that make me a bad person?'

'No of course not, darling. I may have tripped over him when we ran out.'

The Duke takes a left into the street that leads to the hotel and there, in front of us, is the Generalissimo. He is walking in the middle of the road with his hands outstretched like Christ himself upon the cross. A martyr of his own drunkenness and bad behaviour. The Duke doesn't have enough room to get past so he is forced to drive slowly along behind him. A solemn procession. I think the Generalissimo is singing or swearing or something. I see faces in the windows alongside the street. Lace curtains do sharp little dances with our passing.

We make it to the gate of the hotel and the Generalissimo stops walking. He just stops walking and stands there with his arms still outstretched. There is no doubt he means to stop our progress.

The Generalissimo is standing in the gateway. The van is in the driveway. The Duke's behind the wheel. Nothing happens. For a moment.

Something snaps in the Duke. He takes his foot off the break and lightly hits the Generalissimo with the tour bus. The Generalissimo, shocked, falls back and kind of rests for a moment on the bonnet. It looks like he's felt obliged to fall over. He kind of drapes himself on the front of the van like a girl selling a car.

'Can you get out of the way?' shouts the Duke in his best small-town accent.

At the sound of the Duke's voice, the Generalissimo gets up and, somewhat foolishly, moves to the side of the road. The Duke drives smoothly past him and parks.

We both sit for a moment. I find my voice first. 'You realise you just hit the Generalissimo with the tour bus?'

And suddenly we both do.

'He's going to be pretty angry,' I say.

We jump out of the van and in our fear of meeting the Generalissimo on the steps of the hotel and having another confrontation, only this time not armed with a car, we climb into the window of Edmund's room. He is doing his washing with a contented but slightly bored air. He looks happy for the distraction. I'm breathless.

'You wouldn't believe what . . . we . . . did.'

'Forgot your keys?' asks Edmund.

'The Duke hit the Generalissimo with the tour van.'

Edmund puts his washing down. 'Did you kill him?'

The Duke looks shamefaced. 'No, it was just a light tap.'

'With the tour van.'

'Yes.'

'Where is he now?'

'Coming up the front steps.'

I tightly smile from the edge of hysteria. 'Maybe we should stay. Maybe I should stay. You know, safety in numbers. Can I stay over tonight? I don't think I can be alone tonight.' I notice that I am babbling.

There is a knock at the door. We all jump onto various bits of furniture.

'Who is it?' says the Duke in one of his scary voices.

'It's me,' says the Prince.

'Good lord, what do you want?' asks the Duke as he climbs down from the top of the wardrobe. Edmund opens the door. The Prince looks very disconcerted.

'The Generalissimo's locked me out of the room. Can I stay here tonight?'

The Duke doesn't mind one bit. 'Of course, darling.'

Edmund's not so sure. 'It's my room.'

'Surely you won't turn him away,' says the Duke. 'Where else will he go?'

'Your room.'

'I'm not going out there. The Generalissimo might murder me in the corridor. And the corridor is a very painful place to be murdered.'

'So, a pyjama party then,' I say, trying to be cheerful about it all.

Somewhere in the hotel, we can hear banging.

Are we there yet?

The Generalissimo is late. We've been waiting a good hour for him to turn up to the minibus.

'Someone should go and get him,' says the Chancellor.

'Well I'm not getting him,' I say. I'm sure about that.

The Chancellor points to Edmund.

'You go get him.'

'I don't want to get him.'

'I'll go get him,' says the Duchess with the sigh of a long-suffering martyr.

And then the Generalissimo appears at the door of the hotel. He looks awful. Really very terrible. Hungover, dishevelled, unwashed and more than somewhat slightly dazed. He takes a few steps towards us. The motion is more than he can handle. He rushes over to a bin and empties the contents of his stomach. I feel so sorry for the garbage man. The Generalissimo somehow makes it over to the minibus while managing to give the Duke and I the dirtiest looks he can summon from the very darkest places of his soul. He lumbers onto the bus.

'Aren't you going to say something?' says the Chancellor.

'Maybe later,' says the Duke.

We pile onto the bus. The Generalissimo smells like

he died in the night. The Lady puts a tissue to her nose. 'How long is the drive today?'

'Twelve hours,' says the Chancellor.

We all press our hands and faces to the glass in a collective 'Get me out of here' as the van makes its way down the street. The Generalissimo throws up out the window, leaving an aftermath of vomit. We could find our way back to Chieri like Hansel and Gretel by just following the trail of stomach matter.

Rimini

Someone begins to cry. It's the Generalissimo. No one moves to comfort him. After a while the crying stops.

Montegranaro

The hills play hide and seek with the views. The road winds back upon itself again and again until finally the town makes its appearance. And it really is a spectacular walled village. It has stepped out of a lovely age and arranged itself gracefully on a small hill. It is kind on our eyes.

The Chancellor finds the presenter. The presenter says our accommodation is out of town. We follow in convoy through the failing light along a narrow road. We are in complete darkness by the time we reach the villa, which is to be our home while we are here.

We tumble out of the minibus and wheel our bags up the paved driveway. The Chancellor hurries ahead to make arrangements. After an animated conversation with our host, the Chancellor scurries back to us, breathless. 'There aren't enough rooms.'

'Again,' whines the Lady.

The Duchess dumps her bag on the ground. 'Can we stay somewhere else?'

'I asked,' says the Chancellor, wringing her hands, 'but because the festival is on, all of the hotels are full. We have no choice.'

'How many rooms have they got?' asks the Duke.

'They have three.'

'Three,' we all chorus back.

'You're going to have to share beds.'

'Share beds? I'm not sharing a bed,' says the Generalissimo.

'I shouldn't worry if I were you,' says the Duke.

The Chancellor loses control of her bottom lip.

'This is fucked,' says the Duchess.

'Isn't it your job to phone ahead and sort these things out?' says Edmund. 'Or do you need help navigating your job as well?'

Now the Chancellor loses complete control of her face, sits on the ground and starts crying rather noisily.

'There is nothing I can do,' she sobs.

Since the Chancellor is having a minor nervous breakdown on the lawn, the Duke takes the reins.

'All right then, lets have a look.' He strides purposefully towards the available rooms. He comes to the first one. It has two beds. Two double beds. 'You girls can stay here.'

The Duchess has resigned herself to the situation.

'Who's going with who?'

'I'll go with you, Duchess,' I say.

The idea of sharing a bed with a quietly hysterical Chancellor doesn't appeal to me and the Lady likes to sleep nude.

The Duke moves to the second room. It has a double bed. He uses a tone that discourages discussion.

'Edmund, you and the Prince will stay here.'

Next is a small room with a single bed.

'This can be for you, Generalissimo.'

The Generalissimo slouches past and slams the door.

The Duke smiles at his deft organisation of the sleeping

arrangements. Then it occurs to him that he hasn't given himself anywhere to sleep. He starts to walk very slowly and very, very sadly back to the bus.

'Oi.'

It's the Prince. The Duke looks as hopeful as an orphan.

'You can stay with us, you mad old bugger.'

The Duke delightedly skips over to the Prince.

'I knew you wouldn't leave me out in the cold.'

'I hope you don't snore.'

'Of course not, darling.'

The Duke heaves his bag through the door.

—

'He snores.' The Prince slumps worn and tired over his coffee. 'The Duke snores like a freight train. I didn't get any sleep all night.'

The Duke joins us at the table looking bright and refreshed.

'And how did you sleep?' I ask him as he sits down.

'Like a baby. I think that's one of the best nights sleep I've had in ages.' He smiles prettily at the Prince. The Prince smiles back, weakly.

'Show day today and the weather is fine,' says the Duke, ever the optimist. 'It's such a beautiful little old town. It will make a lovely backdrop to the show. How is the Chancellor this morning?'

'She stopped crying. Eventually. The Lady said she was having a bit of a lie in.'

'Well, go and wake her up. We have to get back up to the old town. We're leaving in an hour.'

'I'll do my best.'

I have one last mouthful of coffee before heading off to rouse the Chancellor. Not a job I'm looking forward to. She can be unhelpful at the best of times and these aren't the best of times.

—

'Wake up, Chancellor.'

She doesn't stir.

'Come on, it's show time.'

She kind of snuffles in her sleep. I'm feeling mischievous this morning and she has to get up. No really, she has to get up. I fill a glass with water and after a moment's guilty hesitation, poor the water onto the Chancellor's face. She rolls away from the sodden pillow but still stays firmly unconscious.

'Chancellor?' I check beside her bed to see if she's taken anything. Looks like she has. A mostly empty bottle of sleeping tablets is on the floor.

'For god's sake, haven't you heard of warm milk?'

I race back to the Duke.

'The Chancellor's out cold and it doesn't look like she's going to wake up any time soon.'

'Is she still breathing?'

'Yeah, she breathes. She took some sleeping tablets last night and they are fulfilling their function brilliantly. I can't wake her up.'

'We'll have to leave her. You round the others up and I'll meet you at the bus. Sleeping tablets, my god, hasn't she heard of warm milk?'

'That's what I said.'

'Go!' says the Duke in his scary voice.

It's going to be a tetchy day.

—

We set up, warm up, dress up and make up in record time and still manage to be running very, very late. The audience starts up a slow clap. And then someone starts to chant, I presume, 'why are we waiting' in Italian. The rest of the crowd join in. The evening is warm and perfumed as we walk to the show.

Le Petit Prince

The music begins. The lights snap on. The audience looks up.

Six figures are caught in the glare. The Duke, the Duchess, the Lady, the Prince, the Courtesan and Edmund stand on small planets floating in the air.

The Prince walks out onto a tight rope. It's not fixed to anything at the other end. He feeds the rope out through his hands and places his foot upon it. With each footfall the rope becomes taut and he is suspended in mid-air, stepping into the nothingness, feeding the rope out into the darkness.

A breeze from very far away shifts the tableau, slightly. And then the accident happens.

Something snaps and the Prince begins to fall. But it's not a constructed, theatrical image. He really is falling. He flails his arms uselessly. It takes a good three seconds, three minutes, three hours to find the floor. The floor is your friend. It is always there to catch you. It catches him. It is an unforgiving friend.

He fell as gently as a tree falls. There was not even any sound, because of the sand.

All the lights come on.

We run over to the Prince lying prone on the ground.

He moves a little and groans. A good sign. The bad sign is the way his forearms have new angles in them. He's broken both his arms.

He won't be doing any handstands for a while.

The Generalissimo appears.

'Where the fuck have you been?' yells the Duchess.

'Toilet,' says the Generalissimo.

The Duke, in one graceful move from crouch to impact, hits the Generalissimo fully in the face. The Generalissimo goes down. He finds the floor. The floor is his only friend.

—

We have to send the Prince home. People who are injured fly back first class or get two business class seats. There's the silver lining. At least that's what we tell him. Even if it is not actually true. The Generalissimo also has to go home. We all insist upon it. No one sees him off.

Flight

Somewhere a baby is crying and I have no leg room. Another flight where I get to disembark with bruised knees. And I'm in a middle seat. Two on one side and one on the other. And then the man in front of me puts his seat back and not only does my drink spill into my lap but the chair hits me in the head.

'The correct protocol for reclining seats in airplanes should be part of the safety demonstration,' says the man beside me.

'Couldn't agree more,' I say, suppressing the urge to hit the man in front of me through the headrest. 'I'm not fond of the travelling part of travelling. I like the arriving part of travelling.'

'Going far?'

'Galway. What brings you to this part of the sky?'

'To see family. And you?'

'A gig.'

'What kind of gig?'

I tell him about the company. I always find it hard to explain.

'Carnies,' I begin. 'Show folk,' I continue. 'Aerial dancers,' I finish.

'Sounds like an interesting business.'

'Oh, I don't know. I'm at the tired end of tour. I'm tired of trading on my face. I strike my poses and think it will change the world but no one is saved. We move in unison and think it means something if we keep in time. Living our lives as a series of set pieces. We act like we have forever but we only have now. Drinking ourselves into damnation for an eternal summer. And my body's giving out. And I don't know what comes next. I grow old . . . I grow old . . . I shall wear the bottom of my trousers rolled.'

And I pretend to cry to get the laugh. But then I do for real. Just a little bit.

That's the problem with pretend crying.

'A man's work is nothing but the long journey to recover the two or three great and simple images which first gained access to his heart,' the man says, smiling into his glass.

I want to ask him what his images are but I don't. Instead I tell him about the Prince and then I tell him about Newgrange.

'I've never been to Newgrange,' he says.

'Maybe you can go next year.'

'Maybe.'

'What business are you in?' I ask.

'International trade.'

'Really? What do you trade?'

'Ice-cream.'

'Ice-cream?'

'I like ice-cream.'

'So do I.'

And then he says he needs to go to sleep. He says it was delightful talking to me. The air hostess takes our glasses. I try to watch a movie but can't keep my eyes open.

—

I wake up with a start. I need water. I really need water. I call for the hostess. I look over to the old man. He's slipped in his seat. That looks like an awkward position to be sleeping in. The hostess arrives smoothly to my side.

'Could I, could I, I, I . . . ' I'm stuttering, why am I stuttering? '. . . have some water please.'

'Certainly, Madam.'

She disappears down the human corridor.

The man beside me is still. Very still. Too still. He looks very pale. And very still. Something's missing. What's missing? The rise and fall of his chest. The breath.

I leave the plane for a moment. I leave my body behind. And then the hostess is by my side again.

'Your water.'

I stare at her. I can't move.

'Madam, your water.'

It's like I'm trying to call out in a nightmare.

'Madam?'

I finally find where I left my voice.

'I think . . . I think, the man beside me has . . . died.'

Two big, burly hostesses take the old man to a secret part of the plane. Another two take me to the front. Upgraded to first class. So, that's what it takes. A death on board. It's not worth it. Breakfast is served on china plates. I put the coffee spoon into my pocket. When the tears first hit the back of my eyes, they hurt a little. Now I'm leaking. I cry and cry and then I cry some more and then when I get sick of crying, I start crying again.

—

I avoid the faces of the people waiting at the gate for Loved Ones. I'm not their Loved One so I keep my eyes down. Eye contact would be embarrassing for both parties.

Galway

The sea is green, the hills are green and even the sky is green. Not the sensible, steely blue-green I'm used to but a joyous, lush, show-off kind of green. Stone fences corral winding roads, the sun behind them making lacy shadows. Small houses with tiny doorways crouch low into the land made soft by light rain. Here I am wringing the last moments of pleasure from golden summers, silver summers and now green summers. Summer in Ireland. All two weeks of it.

—

I am standing at the threshold of the smallest hotel room I have ever seen. Pretty much a bed with a wall around it. I reach in and put my case on the bed. I step over the threshold and look for the bathroom. I open a door. It's the wardrobe. Okay. Open another door. Back in the hallway. Feel foolish. Step back into the room. Third door lucky and success. I find the bathroom. The door doesn't open all the way. It gets caught on the basin. I slide into the room. The word water closet comes to mind. A very small room where you get wet. In a corner there is a showerhead and in the other corner, thankfully, a toilet. I go back into the bedroom to undress and then manoeuvre myself around the door. I try to work out the taps. Eventually I do. The water fills the room. I get wet but so does everything else. At least I know the toilet has had a wash down. Shame about the sodden towels. I dress back in the room in the narrow space between wall and bed. I put the case on the floor. Now there really is standing room only. I look in the mirror at my face. The face I deserve. It's not an old face but it is not a young face either. I put on some eyeliner. I take the hairpin bend to the doors. I open a door. Find the wardrobe again. I try one more time and, with a great sense of relief, find myself standing back in the hall.

—

The Duke wrinkles his nose. 'Now that pubs are non-smoking, you realise how bad they actually smell.'

He's right. The bar smells of beer and humans and other things I don't want to properly identify.

'Someone light up a cigarette to mask the stench of humanity for God's sake,' he says to no one in particular.

'I wish I could help you,' I say, 'but it would end in big guys helping me out of the place. Drink?'

'I have been known to imbibe on occasion.'

I try to catch the bartender's eye but I seem to be wearing a cloak of invisibility as far as he is concerned. The Duke reaches over the bar and starts waving his hand.

There are some old guys in the corner breaking into song. They hold each other's hands. In another corner there is a cluster of violins, four men, all in a trance. At the next table women are laughing and falling indelicately about on the couches. We make our way through all the music back to Edmund, the Lady and the Duchess. A worn-looking yet still faintly handsome man is sitting with them at the table.

'They really do sing a lot of the time, don't they?' says Edmund, accepting his drink.

The Duke does the introductions. 'This is our new safety officer to get us though this last season.'

'I'm an old hand,' says the man. He offers me his old hand.

'Pleased to meet you,' I say. But I've met this guy before. He's the guy that would be happy to die on the road. His addiction is to see the next new place. And the next one. And the one after that. And he'll do a good job. We'll be in safe hands. He's an old hand.

The Duke notices Edmund's shoes.

'Nice shoes, Edmund, where'd you get them?'

'The Prince gave them to me.'

'Here's to fallen friends,' says the Duke.

We all toast, being careful to meet each other's eyes in the European fashion.

The Duchess surveys the room. 'Any cute guys here tonight? I'm looking for a Frenchman in Galway.'

'I'm looking for a Greek in London,' says the Duke.

'I'm just in the mood for French men at the moment.'

'You are a manmaniser.'

'Manmaniser is not a word.'

'Yes it is because that is what you are.'

'Hey guys, I've got a joke for you,' says Edmund. 'An Englishman, a Scottish man and an Irishman walk into a bar. The bartender says, "What's this? Some kind of joke?"'

'I'm off,' says the Duke, getting to his feet.

We all decide on having an early night. We pass the

guys with violins. They incline towards each other as if they are sharing a lovely secret. They don't look up as we pass.

We walk back to the hotel through the festival in full swing.

Human metronomes arc, silhouetted by the sky. A group of bell ringers ride in on old bicycles and are flung into the sky, dragged by their ropes sounding invisible bells. A horror puppet show reaches its distasteful climax and the giant monsters made of papier-mâché rampage through the crowd. Apparently Bono is here but I can't see him.

It's been a good night for the balloon sellers. Everyone seems to have one. I watch the balloon that got away turn over and over itself as it lifts into the watery sky.

'Where do escaped balloons go?' I wonder aloud. 'I've never found a lost balloon.'

'Nor have I,' says the Duchess.

'They fall into the sea, says the Duke, 'and join the Great Pacific Ocean Garbage Patch.'

We find ourselves at the Spanish Arch. The Duke sits on the edge of the wall that keeps the bay at bay. The Duchess and I join the Duke on the edge. We kick our legs against the wall. The Lady walks along the edge of the old stone fortification like a tightrope walker. The Old Hand sits a little back from the edge. Edmund stands looking into the middle distance. We each get caught up in our own private musings in a comfortable silence.

'How's the Prince?' asks the Duchess, breaking the reverie.

'He made it home safely,' says the Duke.

'And the Generalissimo?'

'Vanquished.'

'I got a call from my mum this morning,' says the Lady. 'My sister just had her baby. A girl.'

'Congratulations, darling,' says the Duke.

'Thank you. The thing is, I can't help but feel a bit jealous.'

The Duke's eyes sparkle and he laughs briefly to himself. 'All I can say is life is short. Break the rules, forgive quickly, kiss slowly, love truly, laugh uncontrollably, and never, ever regret anything that made you smile.'

The clouds roll above our heads like waves. The sea at our feet, the absolute reflection of the sky. We are bathed in a luminous blue green.

And then Edmund walks up behind the Lady and lightly pushes her into the sea.

'Tell your mother I saved you,' he says, while momentarily forgetting to catch her. He has missed the vital piece of timing in the crucial part of the joke. By the time he remembers, she is out of reach. She slips through his hands and falls into the sea below. She makes a big splash. The Old Hand springs to his feet, shrugs off his coat and jumps into the water after the Lady. She's struggling in the water. Maybe she's been winded. The Old Hand retrieves the Lady in a few powerful strokes and boosts her up the smooth wall high enough so that the rest of us can drag her back onto the bank.

The Duke takes off his coat and wraps it around the Lady. 'Gave us a bit of a turn there, darling.'

I can see Edmund behind the Duke looking most sorry and he says as much. 'I'm so sorry . . . I didn't mean to . . . actually . . .'

'We'll flog Edmund later,' says the Duke. 'We'd better get you warm first.'

'M . . . M . . . My heart. Very fast,' says the Lady.

The Duke smiles. 'Your heart beats a symphony throughout your life. Sometimes slow, sometimes fast. It's okay. You're not dying yet.'

In our concern for the Lady we forget about the Old Hand. Fortunately he's found the stairs further down the quay and walked himself out of the sea. He looks like a very cold and sorry entrant in a wet T-shirt competition but certainly in good nick for a man of his age.

We all hurry the Lady to the nearest taxi.

There is an art, or, rather, a knack to flying

It is a grand albeit fresh morning. I'm tired. I can feel just about every muscle that encases my bones. My body is discordant chord of tight sinew. I have a go at trying to touch my toes. They seem very far away this morning.

Edmund runs up, breathless. 'The Lady is down.'

'Down. What do you mean down?'

'Stomach bug. Finally ate something. Doesn't look like food agrees with her. Can't leave the bathroom. She is down and out.'

'Stomach bug? Not the flu? After her impromptu swim in the river?'

'Alright, yes, she has the flu but I don't think it has anything to do with last night.'

'You keep telling yourself that, my friend.'

'I will.'

'You should.'

'I do.'

'I'm glad.'

'I'm going.'

'Alright then.'

Edmund turns to leave but says instead, 'I feel bad.'

'I know.'

Edmund looks positively distraught for a moment.

'What's the secret to comedy?' I ask.

'I don't know, what's the . . .'

'Timing.'

Edmund laughs like a mad man and we make our way to the site.

—

I'm doing the Lady's role for the next show. We lose one more performer and the show won't go on. I'm checking the gear with the Duke. He tries to catch my eye.

'All right?'

'All right.'

'How you going to be for the shows?'

'Fine. I've done the part before. No big deal.'

'I've double-checked the rig.'

'Glad to hear it.'

And he puts his hand on my shoulder. There is a soft thudding sound. I stay very still, pinned to my chair. He takes it away just before I fall apart.

I'm feeling scared. I'm scared about doing the show, feeling awful about this thing I love doing. Who on earth would want to watch me running around? Look at me, the kid who never came in from playing in the back yard. This worried longing: I can't wait for it to begin and I can't wait for it to end and I always want it to be great. That's the problem with live performance. You have to be great over and over again. It's a bit like life.

I slouch off to warm up.

There are two kinds of pain, my old trainer would say

to me. Good pain and bad pain. Good pain goes away when you stop doing the thing that is causing you pain but bad pain stays after you have stopped doing the thing that was causing you pain. That's how you know when you are injured. Looks like I'm injured then. There is something sharp deep in my hip. So deep I can't touch it. The injury winds down my thigh, through my knee, coils around my calf and attaches to the instep of my foot. It is like a snake that entwines my leg, with its tail in my instep and its head deep in my hip. I contort myself into new postures to try to find the way to stretch the reptile away. The problem with living in the material world, when pain becomes just another sensation, is that you get very good at denial. Pain is acceptable if it doesn't get in the way of the activity to be performed, especially if it's a creeping injury that arrived without the big entrance of an accident. A niggle that soon becomes a familiar companion. And then other muscles get involved in the act and try to hide the betrayer, the weak fibre, the one hanging from a thread. And then suddenly you get the fear you didn't know you had. The body becomes scared before the mind realises it but then pushes the action through anyway. And different injuries make you feel different ways. Shoulders make you feel small and pathetic. Hips make you afraid and backs stop you in your tracks. And hands, hands are complicated.

Edmund lightly dances over to me. 'Still playing up?'

'Playing up?'

'The dodgy hip. Can I help?'

'You can put an elbow and all of your weight just here if you like.'

I roll onto my front. Edmund eases his weight into my body. His bone separates muscle and sinew. I surrender to the intense sensation. It hurts. I resist flinching. He reaches the centre of the injury and all the pain gives way and I enter a distinctly euphoric state. A great sense of peace descends upon me. It's like once the injury has been touched, really touched, a hard touch, it goes away. Edmund eases his weight off, kisses me on the head and rolls away. I find my way back onto my feet the long way round.

—

I look at myself in the mirror. I still look like me but tired all the time. Looks like I'm going to get the face I deserve. I want my other face. I gratefully reach for the white base and erase myself with long strokes of the sponge.

—

There is an almost imperceptible hesitation on everyone's part before they climb the rig to begin the show. Edmund does an extra couple of push-ups but then is straight up. He climbs easily and quickly. The Duchess looks like she says a quick prayer before she gracefully leaps off the ground. The Duke stubs out his cigarette and steps up. He ascends with an even pace. The Duchess gets a couple of body lengths up the scaffolding, turns upside down into a stunt and smiles at me.

'You coming?'

I can't stand up straight. The muscles say no, not this time. Climbing has become scary. The bruises are getting in the way. I'm as weak as a very small and very weak thing. And there it is. The fear. I don't want to go up. I put my hand on the scaffolding.

—

The music begins. The lights snap on. The audience looks up.

Four figures are caught in the glare. The Duke, the Duchess, the Courtesan and Edmund stand on small planets floating on the air.

Edmund walks out onto a tightrope. It's not fixed to anything at the other end. He feeds the rope out through his hands and places his foot upon it. With each footfall the rope becomes taut and he is suspended in mid-air, stepping into nothingness, feeding the rope out into the darkness.

I'm high up, ready for the first cue, leaning out into the darkness. Ready to leap out into the void. I breathe. My first cue comes and goes. I don't move. I've forgotten how to move. In short, I am afraid.

Someone calls my name. I look across. It's the Duke.

'GO. NOW!'

I throw myself at the ground.

And miss.

—

We all survive. We give form to feeling. We lose our identity in the roles and it's a good thing. It's good to hide in someone else for a while. The sweet forgetfulness of being someone else. We swim in the sea green sky. Playing in the arc between two deaths.

'til human voices wake us, and we drown

We made it work. The final show. We feel the only way you can feel after doing a show. Alive.

We pack up in record time.

'Well done everyone,' says the Duke as he loads the last piece of equipment onto the truck. 'I propose we go back to the hotel, get cleaned up and meet at that bar we found last night.'

We disperse tired but enormously pleased with ourselves.

—

Three Australians and a New Zealander walk into a bar looking fabulous. We pause at the door for effect. The room does not stop talking to look at us but we pretend they do anyway. The Duchess leads a subtle posing sequence that would not look out of place on a catwalk. She is wearing towering heels and a piece of material so skimpy it is the mere suggestion of a dress. It narrowly affords the semblance of modesty for the bits, the Duchess is required by law, to be modest about. The

Duke wears his velour suit with aplomb. Only this guy can get away with velour. Edmund wears architectural jeans and I'm in a clever red dress I picked up in Rome. No one in the bar is in the least bit interested. Tough crowd. The Duke points to a free table and we set off. Edmund falls over a chair and ruins the sophisticated effect we were all trying to create. I guess when you know you're graceful, you don't mind being awkward.

We pass the guys with the violins we saw the night before. They don't look like they've moved since the last time we saw them. Maybe they live here.

We settle around the table and place our drinks down. Nothing feels as exhilarating as doing a show but alcohol keeps the feeling going for a while. And sex. And dancing.

'I'm going to dance,' says the Duchess. Not that anyone else is dancing but such details never disturb the indomitable Duchess. 'Come on, Edmund.'

I finish my drink and suddenly feel overwhelmed with tiredness. I look at the Duke. He looks weary.

'So you coming to Newgrange with me tomorrow?' I ask. 'I was thinking we could take the bus at about nine-thirty or ten?'

'Oh darling I totally forgot all about that. I have to stay here and make sure the gear gets to Ghent. I can't possibly go with you. I am so sorry.'

I try not to look disappointed.

'Now don't give me that look. There's nothing I can do.'

'I know, I know.'

An awkward silence settles between us.

'I'm exhausted,' I finally say. 'I'd better get going.'

'Of course, darling. I'll see you at breakfast.'

As I walk down the cobblestone street, the car alarms sing to me.

I have heard the cars singing, each to each.
I do not think that they will sing to me.

A blue circle

The breakfast room is busy this morning. The Duke, the Duchess and Edmund are already at a table. I join them. We call tired 'mornings' to each other and concentrate on our coffees. The Lady appears at the table.

'Feeling better?' says Edmund.

'Yes, better, thank you.' She looks paler and hungrier than usual. She puts nine small jars of jam from the breakfast bar on the table beside her.

'What are the jams for?' asks the Duke. 'Are you expecting to have a long breakfast this morning?'

'They're for presents for people back home. Wrap them up, put a ribbon on them and they'll look lovely.'

'That's worse than re-gifting.'

'What's wrong with re-gifting?'

The Duke frowns.

'I've met someone,' says the Lady.

'How did you manage to meet someone from your sick bed?' asks the Duke.

'It's the Old Hand. We got to know each other while I was confined to my bed. He looked after me.'

'Talk about never letting on opportunity pass.'

'He's German. I might move to Germany with him. He lives in Ludwigshafen. I hope he wants kids. I'm very fertile. I once got pregnant on the pill, with a diaphragm while using a condom. He seems very nice.'

'I don't know if I could live in a country where you get yelled at by little old ladies for jaywalking,' says Edmund. 'They can't sing and they can't tell jokes. The Germans are being nude now. The Germans are singing now. The Germans are being funny now. Do you want to hear a German joke?'

'No I do not,' says the Lady, suddenly all prim.

'I do,' I say. 'Tell us your German joke.'

'What's a red square?'

'I don't know, what is a red square?'

'A blue circle.'

The Lady laughs for a good five minutes. The rest of us regard her curiously.

'Hey, look what I got,' says Edmund. 'Some girls gave me their numbers after the show.'

The Duke reaches for his coffee. 'That's unusual.'

'Yeah, no, but look.' Edmund holds a square of paper in his hand.

The Duke sniffs. 'Very impressive.'

'Yeah, no, but look.'

He lets go of the bottom of the square and a concertina of phone numbers fall from his hand. At least fifty teenage girls have organised themselves into a neat list of phone numbers. Edmund beams at us. The Lady takes a sip of water.

The Duke toasts Edmund. 'We all want to be like you when we grow up.'

'I want to be funny. Am I funny?' asks Edmund.

'You are. You're very odd,' says the Duke with small gesture of his head. 'Now,' says the Duke, fixing me with his mercurial eyes, 'I have found a chap who is driving to

Dublin this morning. You can go with him. Much more comfortable than a bus. He's called Sean.'

'Why are you going to Dublin?' asks the Duchess.

'I have to catch a train to Newgrange.'

'What's a Newgrange?'

'It's a place where I get to stand in a stone room and watch the sun come up.'

'Sounds exciting. What are you going to do after that? Stand in a field and wait for it to rain? You're too wild for me.'

'Where are you going next?' I ask the Duchess.

'Back to Berlin to catch up with my fabulous friends. I'm going to move there next summer.'

'Edmund?'

'Moscow. I hear the women are beautiful there.'

'What about your girlfriend back home?' asks the Lady.

'Broke up ages ago.'

'By email?'

'Text.' Edmund manages to look ashamed.

The Duke puts his hand on my arm. 'You are going to come and stay with me in London after you finish in Newgrange, aren't you, darling? You can finally meet Ivan. We'll find somewhere in the old ranch to put you.'

'I'm looking forward to it,' I say. And I am.

The Duke's phone starts ringing. 'Excuse me. It's the office,' he says as he moves away from the table.

'I've got a joke for you,' says Edmund.

'No more jokes. None of them are original,' I say.

'Just one more. A grasshopper walks into a cocktail bar and the bartender says, "Hey, do you know there is a drink named after you?" And the grasshopper says, "What, Kevin?"'

The Duke comes back to the table with an ashen face.

'What's wrong?

'The company's folded.'

———

When we say our goodbyes in the foyer we are distracted. We stand close to each other one last time. 'See you . . . soon,' we say, unsure that we will.

The Duchess is wearing an original creation. She looks like a Technicolor pirate in high heels.

'A parrot would really finish off that look,' says Edmund.

'Do you think I should get a parrot?'

'No,' I say too quickly.

'You must come and meet all my friends and be fabulous with me in Berlin,' says the Duchess.

'I'm looking forward to it,' I say. And I am.

The Lady is struggling with her enormous suitcase. She has added two more to the collection. Such a small woman, so much luggage. One of the zips on one of her suitcases is open.

'One of the zips on your suitcase is open,' says the Duke.

'Thank you.'

The Lady tries to close the case but the zip gets stuck and she accidently sends it the wrong way. Toothbrushes, towels, soap, every imaginable hotel toiletry item and a bathrobe cascade onto the floor. We all help her get it back in the case and the mystery of the suitcases is solved.

I stop Edmund before he gets on the bus.

'I never.'

'You will.'

'You wish.'

'You wish.'

We invoke wishes on each other for a while.

'I hope you meet a beautiful Russian woman who breaks your heart.'

'I'll do my best.'

—

The Duchess, The Lady and Edmund hang out the windows of the coach. The Duke pretends to be a crowd of people reaching for their hands.

We wave until the bus is out of sight.

I turn to the Duke. 'So the Office really said folded? Not solvent?'

'The word they used was bankrupt.'

I decide to commit to a total state of denial until I get to Newgrange.

Newgrange

'Sean?'

The tall, painfully thin man turns around. His face is a collection of angles. The angles become acute in places to fashion a smile.

'I am.'

'I believe you've been kind enough to offer me a lift to Dublin.'

'That's right.'

'That's very good of you.'

'Don't mention it.'

We stand just smiling at each other for a while.

'Well, I'm all packed and ready to go,' I say, gesturing to my suitcase.

'I'll just get some lunch and we'll be on our way.'

I look at my watch. It's 9.30 in the morning.

'Of course, no problem,' I say. The sun is not going to wait for me.

'I know a place just down the way.'

I follow him, trailing my case over the cobblestones.

—

The place is just down the way, around a corner, under

a bridge, over a main road, through an alleyway, around another corner and down a street. Finally, Sean stops at a doorway.

'Just here,' he says with a small smile.

A small café that looks very much like a lot of small cafés we passed on our journey is nestled between two large buildings. We go inside. The smell of frying perfumes the air. We find a table near the window.

'You hungry?' asks Sean.

'No I'm right.'

'Well I could eat a horse.'

—

Two hours later and Sean is mopping up the last of the gravy from his plate. He may well have eaten a horse and if the rider were around, Sean would be chasing him around the table. The service was slow, Sean's appetite prodigious and now it's 11.30 am and we've gone nowhere.

'Right then,' says Sean as he wipes his mouth with a napkin, 'you just wait here and I'll go and get the van.'

Grateful I don't have to lug my bag around Galway again, I readily agree.

—

An hour later, Sean pulls up in a van that looks like he's just picked it up from the wreckers. An ominous cloud billows from the exhaust pipe. I heave my bag into the back and climb in beside him.

'Off we go then,' says Sean.

The van stalls. He tries to start it again. If a car could

cough, then this van has pneumonia. After a couple of attempts, we finally pull away from the footpath.

The landscape in Ireland looks kind of familiar. Not the green aspect of the landscape, the cleared aspect. It's all been cleared like Australia. Ireland holds the dubious honour of being the most deforested area in Europe. Sean tells me the hedgerows, which are the hedges that border the winding road we're driving down, were traditionally used for demarcating land boundaries. Now they act as a refuge for native wild flora and fauna and stretch across the countryside preserving the remnants of the ecosystem that once covered the island. When he says remnants, I suppose he means birds, mice and insects. I can't imagine deer living in a hedgerow.

'Now this is interesting,' says Sean. 'See that tree?'

We are negotiating a roundabout with a small unimpressive tree, which, if asked, I would have called a bush, at the centre of it.

'Yeah.'

'That's a Hawthorn and the Hawthorn is the fairy tree. It is extremely unlucky to cut down a lone Hawthorn, as the fairies will take revenge. They diverted the highway to avoid this one partly because of the public outcry and partly because they couldn't find a single soul in all of Ireland who would cut it down.'

'No way,' I say.

'I heard of a chap with the electricity board and he cut down a fairy tree and the next day he fell off an electricity pole and was killed. Of course, it could have been a coincidence but he had been climbing electricity poles for twenty years without any previous trouble. And then there was the woman in Dublin whose husband cut down a fairy tree and the next day woke up blind. And I knew another man, a farmer who lopped off a branch from a fairy tree to make way for a haystack and lost thirty head of cattle, a sow and four horses.'

'Have you ever seen a fairy?' I ask.

'I've never seen one myself but my father says he did. He saw them riding on the back of sheep on the hillside. I don't know if I believe these things myself but when that big storm hit last year, that tree survived when hundreds were blown away.'

'I'm surprised the fairies don't go for something a little more majestic. You know like an oak or something.'

'Ah well, it's hard to know the minds of the little people.'

We travel along in silence for a while.

'Would you mind if I put the radio on?' I ask.

'Doesn't work, I'm afraid, but I could play the harmonica for you.'

'You play the harmonica?'

'I do.'

And to my thinly veiled horror, Sean produces a harmonica from his pocket and proceeds to play 'Danny Boy' as he drives along the winding road steering only with his knees. Although my death seems imminent, I feel like it would be impolite of me to ask him to stop. I mean, the driver always chooses the music. I stare out the windscreen willing us to survive the roads that seem to turn back on themselves. I can't die in a road accident. I haven't been to Newgrange yet. 'Danny Boy' finishes and I think momentarily that I'm going to survive this after all but then he starts a jaunty rendition of 'When the Saints Go Marching In'. Now I can't die in a road accident because I don't want the last thing I hear to be 'When the Saints Go Marching In'. This cannot be the soundtrack to my death. Sean finishes with a flourish. I'm saved! I will survive. But no. He gives me a rakish smile and then proceeds to play Pachelbel's Canon. My god he's playing Pachelbel's Canon on the harmonica? I can't help but be impressed. He navigates the difficult tune all the while steering with his knees until it happens. Sean misjudges a hairpin turn and, in a moment, we're in the hedgerow. Fortunately we weren't going all that fast.

'All right?' asks Sean.

'Yeah. I'm okay. You all right?'

'Yeah, but I seemed to have lost my harmonica.'

We climb unsteadily out of the van. The front is all mashed in. This vehicle won't be going anywhere ever again. I feel sorry for the van in the way I feel sorry for objects sometimes.

'So what do we do now?' I ask, frantic on the inside because I have somewhere to be.

'Don't know,' says Sean.

I make a decision. I can't wait.

'I'm sorry, Sean, I have to be at Newgrange by dawn. I'm going to have to keep going.'

'That's okay. I understand,' he says understandingly.

I retrieve my case from the van after a brief struggle and turn to Sean. 'Well, thanks for the lift.'

'No problem.'

I wander off down the road with my arm out. When I look back, Sean is still surveying the wreckage.

Athlone

A car pulls in front of me as if to prevent my escape. There are two young men in the car.

'Need a ride?'

I hesitate. Two to one. Maybe I should wait for a woman driving on her own. I have developed a personal set of principles for accepting lifts while I have been waiting by the side of the road. A numbers game. Two young men seem to be too many young men in the car, according to my calculations.

'It's okay, we're Christians,' says the driver, a pudgy guy with shifty eyes.

'Do you have a card or something to verify you're Christians?'

That is the dumbest thing I have ever said. The guys don't seem to notice. The passenger, who is an average looking guy with glasses, speaks up.

'We're from the Dublin Church of Christ. We can take you as far as Innfield.'

I've been walking for half an hour with no luck. It would seem rude of me to refuse. I follow my bag into the back of the car.

'I'm Mark,' says the passenger, 'and that's David over there.'

David turns and gives me a smile I don't entirely trust.

Mark and David proceed to tell me all about their church. I feign interest. Baptism seems to be a big deal to these guys. They talk about the Day of Pentecost and something about an Ethiopian Eunuch. They move onto the Soul of Tarsus. I can't make it out in the accent. They ask and answer their own questions. What was Soul to do? He was told to arise and be baptised. Why? To wash away his sins. Was Soul going to be forgiven of his sins until he was baptised? No! They sound like a very damp congregation. And then they move onto the hallelujah this and Jesus saves that. I am bored and slightly frightened by these two. They deliver their sermon to the approaching road.

David turns north. Dublin is east of Galway. A sign says Ballynagore. This is not right. A voice in my head says, 'This would be an embarrassing way to die now, wouldn't it?'

'Where are you going?' I say loudly, cutting Mark off mid-word.

David looks like he's been caught out doing something he didn't want to be caught out doing. Mark is genuinely confused.

'Yeah, what are you doing, David, this isn't the way to Dublin.'

'I . . . ah. I thought there was a service station along here.'

He throws a quick u-turn and we're back on our way. The signs finally say Innfield and I get out of the car with a profound sense of relief. Mark and David talk about God for a while and then finally look like they are leaving. David turns to me before he gets in the car.

'Before I found Jesus Christ our saviour I would have

picked you up back there, taken you to a quiet back lane and . . .'

'Okay then, bye.' I hurry away.

Innfield

The view from the truck is grand. The driver seems all right. Not that I can make out much of what he says, his accent is so thick. I nod and smile and laugh anyway. The driver says something that sounds like 'The wind never blows in the direction the ship wants to go.'

'I've never heard a truer word spoken,' I say.

Dublin

I've made the last train from Connelly Street at 11.20 pm. I throw myself through the doors like the platform is a sinking ship. As the train escalates, gently I wash back into the seat in a deluge of sensation.

Drogheda

The sign says Drogheda, It's 1.16 am and it is very, very cold on the platform. I suspect this will become the theme of the evening. I cannot find a taxi. Newgrange is a three-hour walk from here. I begin to walk. I must get to Newgrange.

The moon looks unwell. This morning it is a frail, anaemic moon with barely the strength to lift its face from behind the clouds. I have the impulse to throw my bag into a field and be done with it. I resist.

Cold to my bones. I understand cold to the bones now. To the bones. I am cold to the bones and limping from the hip. A dishevelled and grotesque figure, lame, travelling the corralled byways of the damp country, dragging her things behind her. Not that I'm feeling sorry for myself. Time slows and then disappears altogether and there is just the walking, the road and the suggestion of a moon. And the cold. This is cold with a personality. Not a very nice personality. It is an insidious visitor who will not leave my body.

And then like a beacon there is the Tourist Information Centre. I am Lazarus with a suitcase.

The hour before dawn

It's 8 am and rain is falling in the Boyne Valley. The sickly moon flickers in and out of the cloud cover and then finally sputters out. It is moist and cold. The dark begins to develop a texture and the standing stones become more defined with each passing moment. It doesn't look like the sun is going to come out today. People dot the small hillock. The lucky ones who get to go inside the tomb gather around the entrance. The group is impressively good-natured considering the dull early morning. There are seasoned solstice watchers, professional archaeologists and members of the general public like me. Everyone is checking his or her watches with a newly acquired compulsion to know the time. Everyone's eyes are searching the sky. Everyone is concentrating. Everyone is willing the sun to come out except the television crew, who is looking bored.

We get the sign that we can go inside. I leave my case against a wall and hope it will be there when I get back. I show my ticket and make my way into the chamber. I duck my head at the doorway and follow the passage, which inclines for about two metres. As I walk to the centre, the doorway aligns with my feet, which is aligned to the horizon.

There is graffiti in the centre chamber of the tomb. Some of it in languages I can't read but I can read one very large name, pride of place, in the middle of the smoothly crafted stone. It says 'T.B. Naylor 1891'. 'Was here' is implied. Over a hundred years later and we all know that T.B. Naylor was a vandal. Thousands of people realising you are an idiot long after you have died. Hell of a thing to leave for posterity.

Everyone's in and they turn out the lights. Silence descends quickly upon the group. It is so black in here. I mean really black. I have never been able to not see through so much black. And we wait. Sunrise is at 8.39 am. Must nearly be time. And we wait. Someone shuffles his or her feet. And we wait. A little cough somewhere in front. And we wait. I think I hear someone sigh to my left. And we wait.

A voice perforates the nothingness. 'We apologise for the inconvenience.'

Doesn't sound promising.

The voice continues. 'As the sun will not be coming out today, we will be using the lights to show you the effect the sun would normally be making today if there were not so much cloud cover.'

The chamber seems to get slightly bigger as everyone lets out a collective breath of disappointment. I think I hear someone mutter something about the 'fecking weather'.

After a moment a warm glow insinuates itself into the chamber. It lengthens slowly along the floor and a shaft of pure man-made luminescence penetrates the Neolithic monument two metres short of the back wall. It takes seventeen minutes.

A sleight of the light. It's not real but I suspend my

disbelief. Right time, right place and if I didn't know any better, I would have believed it was the sun. And it is better than just standing around in the dark. It is better than nothing. There is the mark against my life. A shaft of light against a spider in the corner of a doorway. I feel like I'm having a slow release epiphany.

—

I walk back out into the nothing morning. My case stands innocently where I left it. I pass a teenager wearing a hat that wouldn't look out of place in the Arctic and not much else. As I walk by, she says to her mother, 'Ah well, at least that's the longest night out of the way for another year.'

Dundalk

The sound of the train is comforting. Moving without having to do anything is comforting. The cup of tea in a Styrofoam cup in my hand is comforting. My phone vibrates, giving me a start and I spill the tea in my lap. This is not so comforting.

'Hello?'

'Hello darling.' It's the Duke. 'I'm still packing up in Galway. Do you want to give me a hand? I'll make it worth your while.'

'Okay. But this time I'll take a train. The one that goes from Dublin to Galway. Direct. The one I planned to get to Newgrange in the first place.'

'Sean not work out? Oh I'm sorry to hear that. Did you get to the passage tomb on time?'

'Just.'

'See you soon.'

And the phone goes dead I can't read the expression on my face in the reflection of the train window. I finish the lukewarm tea.

The Spanish Arch

I find the Duke at the Spanish Arch where we performed what turned out to be our last show. He's hauling lead into the back of a truck. When he sees me he holds out his arms. It's an embrace minus his hands encased in lead-covered gloves.

'Wonderful to see you,' he says and holds on for a moment too long.

I gently extricate myself. 'So the show's really over? The show doesn't go on?'

'Everyone on the board has resigned. We've been in the red for some years now. There was some overspending a couple of years back. The Prince's accident didn't help. And the exchange rate is just awful for exports at the moment.'

'Is there anything we can do?'

'We can go back to project work. Scale things back perhaps. It's hard being based so far away from the rest of the world.'

'Australia, the great backyard of the planet.'

'Quite. A very big backyard far away from the main house.'

'You have any spare gloves? I could do with some heavy lifting just now.'

'Over by the case.'

I find some gloves and start moving the lead. 'What do you think is going to happen to everyone?'

'Let's see. The Lady will be married with children by the end of the year. The Prince will also start having kids, possibly by accident. The Duchess will become a celebrated performance artist and Edmund will move into musicals. The Princess will turn up on the news one day either as a missing person or at the centre of an international incident.'

'What about the Chancellor and the Generalissimo?'

'I don't care. Do you?'

'Not at all.' I drop another heavy brick onto a pallet. 'And me. What do you think will happen to me?'

'Anything you like. But you're probably too old to become an astronaut now.'

'And you?'

'Something always comes up.'

We move heavy things without speaking for a while, lost in our own thoughts.

Maybe our predictions about the others will come true but, for the moment, no one is entirely sure what to do. The company is broke because where we come from they are highly suspicious of 'artists' or anyone who says darling for that matter. Anything that doesn't include balls and short shorts is aberrant behaviour. We've only survived this long through pure optimism and grim bloody-mindedness.

'Tom died,' says the Duke suddenly.

'Oh no. No.'

'Yeah. While we were in Montegranaro.'

'I knew that cat. I loved that cat.'

'He went off . . . to find somewhere to . . . somewhere to die.'

'Cats do that.'

'Yeah but . . . Tom the cat.'

'I know.'

'I haven't actually had a chance to grieve about it yet. So I will now,' says the Duke. He pretends to cry. And then we laugh. And then we sing along to 'Bohemian Rhapsody', which is playing over the loudspeakers in the street. Well, we attempt to sing 'Bohemian Rhapsody'. It's a very long and complicated song. We sing it very badly. We give up and go back to laughing.

After we finish packing up we find the nearest bar and drink ourselves into forgetfulness and if you said you saw us with tears in our eyes at the end of the night, we'd call you a liar.

Eire

The dining room is busy, busy, busy and I'm going to have a full local breakfast. Before me on a very large, white plate is bacon, eggs, fried tomatoes, fried mushrooms, fried potatoes, fried bread with butter, baked beans (probably fried), black pudding, white pudding and sausages. I find an empty table and commit wholeheartedly to the sin of gluttony. I feel revived by a night in a warm room. The clean sheets were everything I had hoped for and there is nowhere else I need to be right now but here.

I realise someone is standing at my table, for how long, I don't know. I look up. It's the guy who caught my phone at the airport. Spooky. He's tall and lean and his dark hair cascades across his blue eyes in a most attractive manner.

'Mind if I sit here?' he asks, gesturing to the empty chair beside me in an accent I still can't place.

'Of course, I feel like we're old friends.'

'I beg your pardon?'

'You caught my phone at the airport. A while ago now.'

He looks disconcerted. 'I'm sorry, I don't know what you're talking about.'

'Must have been someone else.' My black pudding is

suddenly fascinating to me. I'm going to try it this time. I feel like I should be able to eat black pudding in the same way I feel like I should be able to eat dog.

We sit in silence for a moment. He smiles.

'I do remember you from the airport,' he says, 'and I saw you on the road in Italy. Didn't you see me wave?'

'No, I missed the wave but I saw you travelling in a much nicer bus than ours.' I pick up a coffee spoon and slip it into my bag. 'I saw your show in Poznan. I liked it very much.'

'Thank you, I saw your show in Bassano. It's wonderful.'

'I didn't see you in Bassano.'

'It was a big event.'

'It was.'

'I saw you in Rome.'

'I saw *you* in Rome.'

'How was the tour?'

'It had its moments. And yours?'

'It was a riot. I started a couple myself.'

'Well done.'

'Such a life, eh?'

'Such a life.' I take a sip of my tea. 'But it looks like the company's finished.'

'I'm sorry to hear that.'

'I don't want it to stop.'

'I know.'

'I like being in the sideshow.'

'It's fun.'

'Maybe it's time to do something else.'

'Like what?'

'I don't know. How's the south of France this time of year?'

'Very pleasant.'
'You got anywhere you need to be?'
'No.'
'What's your name?'
'Kevin.'
'Is it?'
'I'm afraid so.'

And then my body does something while I'm not looking. I suddenly notice my hand isn't where I left it. He doesn't seem to mind.

London

London, where the streets are paved with bitumen. Last time my relations were in London town they were being escorted onto ships bound for the colony. I make a note to myself not to steal any bread while I am here. The forests are long gone and in their place are tall buildings. The sounds of animals and streams have been replaced by multifarious British accents. They sound like birdcalls to me.

I descend into the underworld of the Tube and encounter a group of young Australians standing further down the platform. They sound like crows. They really do. Oh well. Crows are part of the avifauna. London has accents for all occasions. When the train is late, a Geordie accent reports the delay, a BBC Received tells us to mind the gap and a cut glass tells us what to do next.

I make my way back to daylight like Orpheus returning from the underground, emerge from West Hampstead Station and try to get my bearings.

Walking towards me is a familiar figure. We arranged to meet again in London and here he is, the unfortunately named Kevin. He must have another name somewhere.

———

His flat is a converted front room of an enormous house, although all the houses in West Hampstead look big to me. This is where Mary Poppins lives. He makes me a cup of tea, smiling. I can't help but smile too. We're both wearing our best manners. Outside the bay window is England, so familiar yet so foreign. Just like this man standing before me.

We catch up. We get to know each other once more. I map the terrain of his body, the ranges and plains of muscle and bone. He has a worker's physique, a form designed to move the material world, in this instance my body. We find the ways that we fit together, which are numerous, and the way our voices sound together, which is melodious, at least to our ears, and before we know it, the room is cloaked in shadows. Night has crept in and the darkness helps us find stillness and words once more.

'So what are you going to do now?' he asks.

'How about a cup of tea?'

'I mean now that the company's finished.'

'Is the tea still on offer?'

'I can put the kettle on.'

'That would be nice.'

He gets up and goes to the kitchen, which is conveniently located in the corner of the room.

'So? What now?'

'I don't want to go back. I feel like I've met everyone I'm supposed to have met back in the Antipodes.'

He fills the kettle with water. 'There are two kinds of people in the world: those who prefer to say yes and those who prefer to say no. Those who say yes are rewarded by adventure and those who say no are rewarded with safety.'

'I say yes.'

'That makes you brave.'

'If not particularly sensible.'

'Sometimes yes is the sensible answer.'

'I'm glad I said yes to you.'

'So am I.' He meets my eyes briefly and then arranges a teapot and two cups on a tray. 'What do you want to do then?'

'I don't know. I don't have anything to show for all the years on the road and I don't know what to do next. Maybe I should have been spending my time cultivating a clutch of children in a modest house in an obscure suburb at the furtherest, most combustible part of the world, buried alive in a pleasant street no one ever walks along, where no one can hear you scream, perpetuating myself in a vague state of dread, surrounded by a fortress of electricity and plastic, eating the pain, moribund in my huge, immobile body, suffocating the world as I propel myself around in a small moving room with wheels. Maybe that's what I should have been doing.'

'Maybe you should have.'

'Maybe. Maybe. How do you justify a life's work dedicated to balancing on a wire or standing on your hands on an untidy stack of chairs? What kind of person wants to know how many people you can fit on a bike or how many clowns in a small car or how many drummers it takes to make a human mobile? So many years of training and practice goes into it all and it's nothing but written on the wind. It's all written on the wind.'

'It is.'

'My old trainer showed me a photograph of a handstand trick he used to do in China that was so dangerous and detailed that it took ten minutes to set up; a trick that lasted five seconds. Years of training, he said, for five seconds of almost impossible and no one will ever see it again.'

'But you saw it.'

'No. He told me about it. I hadn't been born yet. Apparently it involved chairs and swings and ladders and small children.' I look at my empty hands. 'I hope this hasn't been a waste of time, after all. I just didn't want to live the same life twice, only taller the second time round, around the corner from the first time round. I feel guilty about all of the lives I could have, should have led. There were high expectations of me, great expectations, and I didn't become what they wanted.'

He pours boiling water into the teapot. 'Why not?'

'Because our life is nothing but the long journey to recover the two or three great and simple images which first gained access to our heart.'

'Albert Camus.'

This guy really knows his French Absurdist writers.

He brings the tray over to the bed. 'And they were? These great and simple images?'

'The dress-up box . . . playing just pretend . . . playing in the other world that makes this one easier to understand . . . a little girl in a white tutu and wings made of coat hangers and tulle with silver sequins around the edges . . . and how nice everyone was to me afterwards saying well done and aren't you pretty . . . a room full of people laughing at the same time . . . feeling less lonely for a moment . . . a daddy-long-legs spider in the doorway . . . performing for an imaginary crowd of thousands from my lounge room . . . an interpretive dance, yes I said inter- pretive dance, illustrating the imminent demise of our planet performed by students from the local university . . . I turned my back on safety and security because this is where my heart led me . . . to the wanderers, the ego-tists . . . performing for the abstracted love of a thousand strangers . . . praying at the altar of Dionysius . . . abandoning the banality of life . . . submitting to the chaos . . . this restless existence . . . it's intoxicating this . . . endless summer . . .' I've wound the sheet into a tight, spiralling knot. 'And you know what? I was right. I was right to follow my heart. I had to follow my heart. I couldn't be buried alive in their expectations. I had imagination, a curiosity that needed to be satisfied, and boundless energy. I had hope.'

He kisses me. It takes me by surprise. But, then, I draw back. 'I don't know about my ability to . . . commit.'

'People change.'

'Life's a comedy, at least mine is, and in comedies the characters don't change.'

'People change.'

'Not everyone finds love. Miss Havisham never found peace.'

He hands me a cup of tea. 'Maybe so, but Miss Havisham was a martyr to a single disappointment and a fictional character.'

This guy really knows his Victorian English writers.

'I've given up. Always ends the same. Someone leaves.'

'Well I believe that you can't give up because every morning you wake up and enjoy the miracle that you're still alive, until one day you don't wake up, but by then you're beyond caring. And it's better to wake up with someone at your side.'

'Anyone?'

'Not anyone.'

I pour milk into my cup and reach for the sugar. 'Have you got a teaspoon?'

'No.'

'No teaspoons?'

'I had some friends over and the next day, all my teaspoons were gone. I haven't had time to replace them.'

'Hang on.' I open my bag and produce an impressive pile of teaspoons. More than I thought. No wonder my bag's so heavy.

He laughs. 'For I have known them all already, known them all – have known the evenings, mornings, afternoons.'

'I have measured out my life with coffee spoons.'

This guy really knows his arguably most important English-language poet of the twentieth century.

The pleasures of
staying in bed

There are many.

Acknowledgments

With heartfelt thanks to:

Carrie Tiffany and Edwina Preston for making me
    write to impress them
Chris Thompson for reading it for the first time and
    telling me what he really thought
Vince Leigh, Aoife Holahan, Lucy Nelson, Tracey
    Meszaros, Matt Millikan and Richard Holt for the
    one-liners and the glamour
Varuna for the space and time to not get as much done
    as I'd hoped on the book
Peter Bishop for being an oracle
Writing Australia for inspiring me do another rewrite
Mark MacLeod and Valerie Parv for their good taste
Clare Woods for support at a time I really needed it
Vanessa Roberts for reminding me of a story I'd left out
The team at Seizure for being great at what they do
David Henley for his energy and vision
Caroline Hamilton for being a source of constant
    inspiration

Dayan Warnakulasuriya for making jokes about the
    French
Jonathan Dyer for the various translations, especially
    those in French
Louise Gough for helping me realise I can write a bit
    and also for all of the beer
Roderick Poole for giving me the gig
And the delightful Patrick Allington for going back
    into the story with me one last time and making it
    all better. It was an amazing journey. Thank you.